Aste

PENELOPE LIVELY
Astercote

Illustrated by
Antony Maitland

Mammoth

Also by Penelope Lively

The Driftway
Fanny and the Monsters
The Ghost of Thomas Kempe
Going Back
The House in Norham Gardens
The Revenge of Samuel Stokes
A Stitch in Time
The Voyage of QV66
The Wild Hunt of Hagworthy

First published in Great Britain 1970
by Heinemann Young Books
Published 1996 by Mammoth
an imprint of Egmont Children's Books
Michelin House, 81 Fulham Road, London SW3 6RB

Reprinted 1997, 1998

Copyright © Penelope Lively 1970

The right of Penelope Lively to be identified as author of this
work has been asserted by her in accordance with
the Copyright, Designs and Patents Act 1988

ISBN 0 7497 0793 3

A CIP catalogue record for this title
is available from the British Library

Printed and bound in Great Britain
by Cox & Wyman Ltd, Reading, Berkshire

To
Josephine and Adam

Prologue

THE MAN stood at the cottage door and saw long, black evening shadows stretch across the emptiness of the village street. His body ached with fever and he was so weak that he would have fallen but for the wooden door-frame against which he leaned. He thought it almost certain that he would die that night: with the others, the sickness had taken three days only, and he was now in the evening of the third day. But he had wanted to look once more at the sky, and the trees, and the rise of the field beyond the houses.

He was the last person left alive in Astercote.

The village was quite silent and still, save for the chickens scratching in the gutter down the centre of the street, and an ox, its tether hanging loose from its neck, wandering up and down, confused and frightened by its unexpected freedom. Seeing it, the man thought of his own beasts and moved, slowly, with infinite difficulty, each step more painful than the last, to the cattle-shed which was the second room of the cottage. He loosed the two oxen and the cow and they walked, dazed, into the evening sunlight and stood there uncertainly.

The dog, which had not left his side since the sickness struck him, squatted down on its haunches and watched him patiently. It must have been half-starved, but it made no movement towards the fowls a few yards away, or the piglets nosing at a midden further down the street. The man thought, angrily, that they had been wrong—those who had said that such an animal was too close to the wild

9

and would revert to its own kind in the end. It had never gone near a sheep, though it watched them with yellow eyes and the hairs on its back standing up in a stiff ridge.

Through a gap in the cottages which flanked the street on either side he could see the sweep of the field beyond, already ridged green where the young barley was coming through. He had sown his selions that spring, like any other, but he would not reap them—nor would anyone else in Astercote. Staring at the billowing greens and browns of the trees beyond the field, he wondered if the forest would spread down again, to swallow up once more the plough-land that the men of Astercote had carved out of the wild, yard by gruelling yard, hacked from furze and thorn and sapling, two, three hundred years ago. Or perhaps they would come from Charlton Underwood, or from Long Barton, and claim the land, when the dread of the sickness had lifted.

And then, indistinctly, as his eyes misted over with fever, he saw a spiral of blue smoke rising from the trees, just beyond the close they called World's End, where old Thomas had cleared his own assart, single-handed instead of joining with the other men and sharing out the strips when the work was done, because he wanted free title to the land, obstinate fellow. So there was still someone left —a woodcutter, perhaps, or swineherd after beechmast for his animals, or even Thomas himself. Whoever it was would do well to stay away from the village for a while yet —perhaps never to come back.

The man turned to look at the church, its square tower blazing gold in the evening sunlight, with the rooks tossed around it by the wind. The church had always seemed like a rock in the midst of their insecure lives, and yet in the face of this calamity there had been no answer to their prayers. The priest had been among the first to die.

He was shaking now, from the fever and the chill of the wind that had sprung up as the sun sank. He turned, and

10

dragged himself slowly back into the cottage, for he wanted to die under his own roof and not by the roadside, like a vagrant.

One

THE FIELD between the village and the wood was striped with regular, deep shadows on the grass as the late afternoon sun threw the uneven surface into a sharper relief. The trees of the wood glowed from palest green through to black in the clear light, and birds popped in and out of the hedgerows in a final, end-of-day frenzy of food-hunting. Twenty-five black and white cows munched their unhurried way across the grass, swishing and blowing, and behind them the golden stone of the village buildings shone against the sky. They would be warm to the touch, breathing out the heat of the day.

At one end of the field a girl lay flat on her back, arms and legs spread out, quite still, and at her feet, head between paws, eyes half closed, a small dog, brown and white but for a smear of black over one eye, still and patient as the stone dogs on medieval tombs. Mair Jenkins, twelve years old, away in a glorious dream where time stood still and anything could happen. And Tar, terrier-type dog, breed uncertain, age about three.

At the other end of the field, nearer the wood, somebody was moving very stealthily along the hedge, inch by inch. A boy, eyes screwed up irritably behind thick glasses, taller and broader than the girl, a year or so older. Peter Jenkins, brother of Mair, frustrated bird-watcher.

How could one hope to bird-watch with eyesight like his —9.4 in one eye and 8.6 in the other or whatever it was and glasses that steamed up and slipped down your nose whenever you got hot, and binoculars quite out of the

12

question. He'd been following this brown bird for ten minutes or more now, and every time he got near enough to get a really close look and see if it was a willow warbler or just another wretched sparrow, it fluttered on a few yards. All the same, he couldn't leave it alone—and he'd had one or two triumphs. An almost certain hawfinch in the garden at home, just once, and a possible shrike on a telegraph pole by the roadside, and a pair of spotted wood-peckers, and a probable nuthatch. He glanced back at Mair, and saw a hand swing up to brush a fly off her face. How anyone could spend so much time doing absolutely nothing . . .

And then, just as he realised that he had lost the bird for good in the depths of a hawthorn bush, he caught sight of something out of the corner of one eye. It was just a glimpse, before it dipped down on the other side of the hedge, but there was no mistaking it—that swerving, soaring flight of a bird of prey, a split second's sight of a curved wing and spread tail. He began to move towards the hedge over which it had vanished. It had been dropping down —perhaps onto a mouse or something: he should be able to get a good look at it as it came up again, or even see it on the ground. It had looked interesting—too small for a buzzard, larger than a kestrel, yet certainly a hawk of some kind. He reached the spot where it had disappeared, where the quickset hedge thinned out just enough for him to peer through into the field on the other side. And there, only a few yards away, was a brown bird on a hummock of grass, tearing at something it held in its claws. What a marvel-lous bit of luck! If only he could get right close to the hedge without disturbing it he could get a really good look.

Somewhere behind him there was a familiar rushing, panting noise. He swung round angrily, and there was Tar bounding over the grass towards him, tail up, tongue lolling out, every inch of his small, barrel-shaped body saying ecstatically 'Thank-goodness-there-you-are-I-haven't-seen-you-for-at-least-five minutes.' Bother Mair! Oh, bother her and bother her and worse things than that! He'd told her to hang onto Tar while he bird-watched—the dog always wrecked everything. And sure enough, the hawk had heard him and was up and off, but swooping down low over the hedge, dipping and swerving, so that for glorious seconds he watched it as it swept across the field, with Tar bounding after it, barking hysterically, before it rose steeply up over the wood, hung for a moment above the trees, and then plummeted down again right into the middle of the wood.

Mair had got up and came stumbling across the field,

calling ineffectively to Tar. Peter waited until she was near and then shouted furiously 'Silly idiot! What did you let him go for! I told you to keep him with you, and it was a hawk I was watching and now he's properly scared it off.'

'I didn't mean to,' wailed Mair. 'I just forgot about him and he went to find you. But look! He's going into the wood and he mustn't because we can't go in after him. It's all wired up and no one's allowed. Oh, Peter, *do* something!'

They both began to run after the dog, shouting as they went. But Tar's hunting instincts were well and truly aroused now and clearly there was going to be no stopping him. Seconds after the hawk had dropped down among the trees Tar scrambled under the barbed wire fence that encircled the wood like a frill round a cake, and vanished into the tangled undergrowth.

The children stopped in dismay. 'Well, we can't go after him,' said Peter crossly. 'So we'll just have to wait till he decides to come out. And I shan't see that hawk again. Wretched dog.'

They sat down on the grass to wait, Peter brooding angrily about the lost hawk and Mair wailing about poor Tar getting lost and goodness knows what might happen to him in there and who cares about the old hawk, anyway.

'Don't be daft,' snapped Peter. 'What could happen to him in there? He'll have a smashing time chasing rabbits and come out when he feels like it. Anyway, why's it all wired up? Who does it belong to, for that matter?'

'The farmer on the other side of it,' said Mair, calming down a bit. 'The one they call World's End Farm. Where Betsy Tranter comes from. You know—the girl with plaits in Dad's top class. He's supposed to be an awfully cross man—quite old—and they keep themselves to themselves and don't come much into the village and he won't let anyone go in the wood because there's rare orchids growing there or something. Dad says the old village people are a bit funny about the wood—they change the subject if you start talking about it. Betsy's nice though—Dad likes her, I know.'

'I didn't know he liked some of them better than others,' said Peter, chewing a grass stalk. 'I thought teachers were supposed to feel the same about everybody.'

'Well, he does. He says children are only people, no more and no less, and people are good, bad or indifferent, and it shows lack of—lack of something or other to think otherwise.'

'Discrimination?'

'That's it. Lack of discrimination.'

They had come to live in Charlton Underwood only a couple of months before, from Wales, when their father had been made head of the village primary school. He'd come back from the interview full of enthusiasm. 'You'll like it—really lovely it is. There's the old village round the green, complete with the church and village pond. Looks as though it's been asleep for a couple of hundred years. And then there's all this new part the other side of the road. The estate where we'll live, and the school. And real country all round.'

They'd been waiting for Tar nearly half an hour now, Mair occasionally getting up to prowl up and down beside the fence, calling him. It would soon be dusk: the birds were beginning to quieten down, the shadows had lengthened as the sun sank and finally melted into an overall darkening of the countryside. And as the evening approached, the wood, so silent and secretive during the daylight, seemed to come gently alive, with small rustlings and disturbances in the brambles, and a whispering of branches, broken by the occasional alarm-note of a jay somewhere among the trees.

'This is ridiculous,' said Peter. 'We can't just sit here waiting for him for ever. Mum'll start getting in a state if we don't go home soon.'

'But we can't just leave him. He might be hurt—stuck

16

in a trap or something. And he *never* stays away as long as this.' Mair was nearly in tears.

It was true. Tar was not given to long absences. Rabbit-hunting excursions seldom lasted more than five minutes. Peter looked doubtfully at the wood, and then back towards the village.

'I really think we'll have to,' he began, and then: 'For goodness' sake, Mair, what do you think you're doing!'

For Mair had got down on her hands and knees and was wriggling under the barbed wire, ignoring the damage that was being done to her shirt and the seat of her jeans.

'I'm going to get him. We can't leave him. He might *die* in there—all by himself. I don't care whose wood it is—I'm going in. Ouch! You might help instead of just watching.'

Peter sighed. And no prizes for guessing who's going to get the blame if we're found out and there's trouble, he thought. He unravelled the long strands of Mair's hair that had got caught up in the wire, and followed her into the wood.

At first they were completely barred by dense undergrowth in front of them, but after edging along beside the fence for fifty yards or so they found a thin trail leading off into the wood, bramble-covered but passable.

'Shall I call him?' whispered Mair. A blackbird, rummaging in the leaf-mould, flew off in panic as they passed, and somewhere ahead and above the jay shrieked again.

'No, of course not. We're not supposed to be here at all —you don't want to announce it, do you? We'll just have to hope he hears us, or scents us, and comes. Or that we spot him.'

They followed the trail, twisting and turning among the trees, for several minutes and then, quite unexpectedly, it opened out into a wide, grassy ride, where the trees and undergrowth had receded, and there was sky above their heads again. It was a slightly sunken green road, thick with spurge and young foxgloves, and the spent leaves of blue-bells. The sides were curiously high, uneven and lumpy, with shoulders of stone sticking out of the grass here and there.

Mair caught up with Peter. She was shivering slightly. 'I hope we find him soon,' she said. 'It's creepy. I don't like woods in the evening. I feel as though things might jump out at me.'

'Well, you wanted to come,' Peter pointed out. 'And if anything jumps out it'll probably be Tar. And I feel like giving him a good beating.'

Suddenly Mair stopped dead. 'Ssh! Listen! What's that . . . ?'

From somewhere to their right, deep among the trees, not too near, but not very far either, there came a strange, continuous sound, soft but insistent. It had two notes: a high, delicate whining and beneath that a gentle, flowing rumble. It sounded half animal, half human.

'It's Tar!' breathed Mair, clutching Peter's arm. 'I'm sure it is. It's his pleased voice. It's Tar and he's talking to someone . . .'

They stood still, listening. There was no sunlight to trickle through the leaves now and even the open path on which they stood was darkening. The trees and bushes that lined it turning themselves into indefinable, sentinel shapes. And all around the wood rustled and stirred with little rushing noises among the branches above, and soft scurryings in the thick leaf-mould underfoot.

Mair sat down on a square block of stone, its base hidden in the grass that fringed the path. She was shivering, and staring round her with black, scared eyes. Her long hair, straggling over her shoulders and down her back, was speckled with leaves and bits of twig. She wished most profoundly that she was at home, having tea in the kitchen.

Peter, on the other hand, was now thoroughly interested. Having listened intently for a few minutes to the curious noise, he began to walk cautiously up and down the path, fifty yards or so in each direction, stopping every now and then to peer into the wood and listen again. Finally he came back to Mair.

'It's coming from somewhere in there. There's no path but there are fewer brambles and nettles there. We can wriggle through. Come on.'

'I'm frightened,' she said. 'What's Tar doing? What *is* in there?'

'I don't know—but I'm pretty sure it's a person. Look, are you coming or not?'

Mair hesitated.

'I thought you were so mad keen to rescue poor darling Tar,' said Peter unkindly.

Mair gave him a nasty look. 'All right then, but you go first.'

Stooping low, sometimes down on their hands and knees, they began to edge their way through the thick undergrowth of the wood, with the strange, wordless conversation getting closer and closer with every step they took. Once Mair trod on a dead branch and the silence was ripped by a sharp dry crack, and then almost immediately by a warning growl ahead of them, which died away as the strange voice rumbled on with its soothing, reassuring flow.

Mair seized Peter's ankle to catch up with him. 'That wasn't Tar,' she whispered, an edge of panic in her voice. 'There's another dog there. A big dog.'

'Well, it's as difficult now to go back as to go on. Anyway, I want to see who it is, and I'm blowed if we're going back without Tar now, after all this.'

Another twenty yards or so, torn by brambles and stung by nettles, and they realised that everything was becoming lighter. They seemed to be close to a clearing in the trees, and the conversation was very loud now—Tar's whimpering overlaid by the strange, wordless mumbling. Peter paused to let Mair catch up with him. Only another few yards and they would be able to see into the clearing.

'For goodness' sake be as quiet as you can now. And be ready to beat it quickly if we have to.'

A curtain of low branches was all that separated them now from the clearing. Peter reached up with one hand, and cautiously parted the leaves. Together they peered through and Mair's hand flew up to her mouth to suppress a startled gasp.

It was the animals that held their attention to begin with. Right in the centre of the open space, lying with his head between his paws, whining softly, tail wagging, was Tar, his eyes fixed steadily on someone, or something, in a patch of shadow. And on the far side, squatting down a few yards apart, were two more dogs, stretched out, relaxed but watchful, staring at the same shadow. Alsatians, surely? And yet a curious kind of Alsatian, their legs too long and thin, the ruffs round their necks too thick, their eyes strangely pale and yellow. Mair clutched Peter's arm in apprehension, her muscles tensed to make a dash for it if they moved. But Peter was staring at a bird in wild excitement. It was perched on a low branch at the edge of the clearing, its head hunched down between its shoulders, one mad, golden eye glaring out from the brown feathers and, as he watched, it shifted and shrugged out a stretch of superb, angled wing, shaking it out lazily before settling down again in a different position. A peregrine, was it? Or a goshawk? He'd never seen either—but in any case what was it doing here? You'd hardly expect to find such a creature in the heart of a wood.

And then he saw the owl, a silent domed shape on a branch, white-speckled, one eye open and the other closed. The Great Barn Owl: what a beauty! He could hardly suppress his excitement.

One of the dogs must have got their scent, for he rose to his feet and moved forward, ears pricked, hairs erect, growling softly and looking towards them. But a word from the figure in the shadows sent him back to his place, grumbling in his throat, to lie down again, nose between paws and ears flattened guiltily.

'Quiet, Fang! Quiet, there!'

The man stepped forward, and they could see him properly. He was short and stocky, with a round, intensely weather-beaten face, quite young, ugly, with crude features that for some reason reminded Mair immediately of the gargoyles on the church tower. The hair was long, coarse and matted, with a fringe almost down to his eyes. It didn't look as though it had seen a pair of scissors in years. He wore old, ragged clothes, pieces of cloth round his body in the appropriate places rather than trousers and shirt. They seemed useless, not the purposeful clothes of someone who has to work, and his feet were bare.

There was nothing in the least alarming about him.

Peter coughed awkwardly, and stood up and moved out into the clearing, with Mair hanging back, an anxious eye on the dogs. Tar, seeing them, rolled his eyes in guilt, but stayed where he was.

'I'm awfully sorry we came in the wood,' Peter began. 'I mean, if it's your wood. I know we aren't supposed to, but our dog ran in and he wouldn't come out and we had to get him. I'm sorry if he's been a nuisance. We'll take him away now. Come *here*, Tar.'

The man stared from under the yellow fringe. 'I don't mind 'e,' he said slowly. 'They all comes to me. But you got no right here. 'Tis our wood and no one comes. You'd best go.' His speech was thick and indistinct.

'All right,' said Peter hastily. 'We will.'

Mair, who had been lurking behind him, half hidden in the bushes, stepped forward and the man caught sight of her for the first time. His reaction was electrifying. He shot backwards several yards, an expression of sheer panic on his face, as the dogs advanced, growling dangerously.

'She's a witch!' he shouted hoarsely, pointing an accusing finger at Mair. 'Get away from me, woman! She's got witch-eyes, I can see 'em.' He began crossing himself frantically, mumbling under his breath, while the dogs crouched down in front of him. They looked ready to spring at any moment.

'I'm not a witch,' said Mair indignantly. 'I've got perfectly ordinary eyes.'

'Please call your dogs off,' said Peter. 'They look as though they might attack us at any minute. And she isn't a witch—at least not that I've ever noticed. She's my sister and she's called Mair.'

Reluctantly, the man told the dogs to 'Get back there . . .'

'They're Alsatians, aren't they?' said Peter, determined to be friendly. 'What's the other one called? Fang and what?'

Still with a wary eye on Mair the man replied, slightly less hostile now, that the other one was called The Bitch. Straightforward enough, thought Peter.

'I don't know nothing about Alsatians, or whatever you call 'em. Them's just dogs. We always had dogs like that in the wood, and at the farm.'

Peter had turned his attention to the hawk. Warily, he approached it.

'It is a peregrine, isn't it?' he said excitedly. 'I say—is it yours? It's almost tame, isn't it? Did you tame it?'

To his surprise, the man suddenly became furtive, almost abject. 'You won't tell 'em, will you?' he begged, sidling up to Peter and touching his sleeve. ''Tisn't for the likes of me to keep a hawk—I know that. I know it's the King's chase. But I only fly 'un at rabbits—just once in a while. You won't tell 'em?'

Peter stared at him in perplexity. 'I'm afraid I don't really get you . . .' he said politely. 'Who don't you want me to tell? I mean, of course I won't tell anyone, but I don't really see who'd care. Least of all the Queen, I should imagine. There hasn't been a king for years, you know.'

The man looked at him with total incomprehension. He stretched out his arm and the hawk spread the great wings again and flapped awkwardly off its perch and onto the man's forearm, the talons closing onto it in a perfect circle. It turned its head towards Peter and the round yellow eyes glowed in the twilight.

'He's a beauty,' said Peter admiringly. 'A real beauty. I say—d'you think I could come and see you fly him sometime? I'm very interested in birds, and I just never saw anything like this before. Do you know a lot about falconry?'

The man seemed flattered by the attention. 'I can fly 'un' he said, with some pride, squinting at Peter with eyes that were a curious pale blue under his thatch of hair.

'Where did you get him from?' Peter persisted, 'and get him so tame?'

'I didn't get 'un. 'E come to me with his wing broke, and I cared for 'un till 'e be better. Now 'e don't want to go away. Like old Big-Eyes there.' The man waved at the owl on the branch above their heads, and Peter, looking up, saw that one wing hung awkwardly.

'Are you a vet?' he said with interest. 'Mr—er—sorry, I don't know your name.'

'Goacher.'

'Mr Goacher.'

There was a splutter of amusement. 'I ain't no mister. Just Goacher.'

Mair, not particularly interested in the birds, had wandered away and was exploring the little clearing. There was a shelter, crudely built of leaves and branches, and the remains of a fire surrounded by a circle of blackened bricks. A small chopper and one or two other tools lay around. One of the dogs got up and moved away to drink some water. Mair watched it intently, her face screwed up in a frown of puzzlement. How odd! How really very odd indeed . . .

Then she turned her attention to Tar, stooping to pick

23

him up. 'Nasty, unfaithful little dog,' she hissed under her breath. But Tar cringed away, whining.

'Here, Peter,' she said suddenly. 'He's done something to his paw. I *told* you he might be hurt!' There was blood on the ground and one claw was almost torn off.

'What do we do?' wailed Mair. 'Oh, poor Tar.'

Goacher sidled up to them. 'I'll fix 'un for yer,' he offered. 'I know what to do with 'un. Just leave 'un here for a day or two.'

Mair looked doubtful but Peter whispered, 'It's not a bad idea. He really does seem to be able to do things with animals. Look at the hawk. And Tar likes him.' They looked again at the injured paw: the dog winced and drew away from them.

'All right,' said Mair.

'You'll have to give me summat for the trouble,' said Goacher sharply.

'Oh,' said Peter, taken aback.

He consulted Mair hastily, and they both delved in their pockets. They had five shillings between them.

'Is this enough?' he said, holding out the money.

Goacher squinted at them, and poked the coins with a dirty, square-ended finger. 'I don't want none of those,' he said grumpily. 'What would I do with 'em?'

'Buy things, I suppose,' said Peter. 'That's five shillings, you know—it's quite a lot. Well, what do you want us to give you, then?'

Goacher considered. Then he put out a hand and touched the knife slung from Peter's belt by a length of string. It was a very ancient penknife, the first Peter had ever had, rusty now, missing one blade completely and with the other one half-broken. He only carried it around from long habit—it wasn't much use.

'That?' said Peter in bewilderment. 'But that's not worth anything like five bob. You could buy a new one with the money.'

Goacher stared, stupid-faced. 'I want that,' he repeated, with an obstinate scowl.

Peter untied it and handed it to him. He turned it over and over lovingly, running his finger along the blade.

'What about Tar?' said Mair impatiently. 'How soon will he be better? When can we come and fetch him?' This peculiar man did seem to have a way with animals, she'd decided, and Tar certainly had developed a passion for him. She had sat down on a shoulder of stone that stuck up from the grass at the edge of the clearing, and was scraping idly at the surface with a flint.

'Don't you do that!' said Goacher in sudden anger. 'Leave 'un alone. That be reeve's house. You leave 'un as they be for when they come back. They don't like folks disturbing anything.'

'All right, all right,' said Mair hastily, getting up. Really, he did come out with the oddest remarks. 'When who comes back? What house? Is it some sort of game you're playing?' Though a grown man playing pretend games seemed a bit daft.

'Game?' said Goacher sulkily. ''Tweren't no game when they all died, one after t'other, were it?'

Mair was just opening her mouth to pursue the matter, when a great swelling rumble filled the air, beginning gently and getting louder and louder until the whole sky seemed to throb with noise and the ground to shake under their feet. As it began, Goacher looked up at the sky apprehensively, and then, as it grew louder, clutched in anguish at Peter's arm, and finally, as all the wood noises were drowned in the thunderous rumble, dropped on his knees, crossing himself wildly and mumbling incoherently, 'God 'a mercy, Lord 'a mercy on us all!'

The children stared at him in utter astonishment. The noise reached a crescendo, and began to die away.

'Whatever's the matter?' said Peter.

25

Goacher pointed upwards at the sky. 'A sign . . .' he gabbled. "Tis a sign of things to come. An omen . . .'

'It's not an omen,' said Peter, a trifle impatiently. 'It's an R.A.F. transport aircraft from Brize Norton. They always do low-flying practice at the end of every month. You must have heard them before. Look, there it is.'

Above the trees, like a huge, steady silver fish against the sky, the aircraft was sliding away to the south, seeming to be quite detached from its own noise.

'I can't see nowt,' said Goacher obstinately, staring straight at it. 'I don't know what yer mean.'

Peter gave up. There were moments when communication with this strange creature broke down altogether.

'Never mind,' he said. 'When shall we come for Tar, then?'

They arranged to return in two days' time. Goacher had picked Tar up and was talking to him in a crooning, senseless mumble. It was twilight now and they could only just make out the dark shapes of man and dogs: they looked very much a part of the wood, as though it had grown up around them. Following an easier trail back to the main path that Goacher had shown them, they hurried away.

They didn't speak until they were out of the wood and walking across the field again towards the village.

'I'm starving,' said Peter. 'Absolutely falling apart. I hope Mum's got masses of tea ready. What a funny man that was . . . But I'm sure he'll see to Tar all right, and we wouldn't have known what to do about his paw, and there isn't a vet in the village, far as I know. I say, though, we'd better not mention we went in the wood when we get home. Say we left Tar with a friend or something. Come on, Mair —we're late already. What on earth's the matter?'

Mair had stopped, and was staring back at the dark, silent mass of the wood, black against the violet sky, an island among the fields that lapped gently all around it. The countryside was so quiet now, and yet she had this

26

odd feeling that somewhere, unseen, secret, there was a busy, throbbing life. She blinked and shook her head violently: it was as in one of her daydreams now, she was sure she could hear noises. A creaking, bumping noise, like a cart going along a track—but there was no track. And the soft thump and swish of cattle passing—but the cows had long since been taken in for milking. And, stranger still, the faintest sound of church bells ringing, but not from the village ahead, from somewhere behind them. From the wood.

'Can you hear bells?' she said abruptly.

Peter stared. 'Are you daft?' he said.

Mair shook her head again, and the noises went away. The wood was just a wood, and the field a field, and there were midges biting her ankles.

'Yes, it was peculiar,' she said. 'But do you know what was the peculiarest thing of all? Did you see what those dogs were drinking out of?'

'No. What?'

'It was a font,' said Mair slowly. 'A stone church font—just the bowl part of it. Where on earth do you think he got that from?'

Two

THE WOOD hummed and sang, life flickering and rustling at every level: insects underfoot and at knee-height, dappled moths, bees, butterflies, birds above and around, small ones flitting neatly from branch to branch, pigeons crashing noisily overhead. Sunlight crackled down through the leaves, dust spinning in the yellow shafts. A squirrel poured soundlessly down the trunk of a tree and vanished into the brambles: somewhere ahead a woodpecker thumped. It was a busy place, preoccupied with its own affairs.

The children had come back to collect Tar, but so far they had been walking twenty minutes or so with no sign of Goacher. They had found the wide track again and began to walk down it, searching for the trail that had led to the clearing. Peter thought irritably that he should have marked the spot—it could take them ages to find it again, with nothing to guide them. He thought of shouting, and then decided that would be unwise. After all, they weren't exactly clear at the moment who Goacher was. It seemed obvious that he must have something to do with the farmer who owned the wood, but all the same nobody had said yet that it was all right for them to come there, so it didn't seem a good idea to advertise their presence.

And then Mair, turning round to look behind her, let out a stifled scream.

Fang—or was it The Bitch?—was standing in the middle of the track, twenty yards or so behind them. He looked very handsome, the fawn and grey of his coat standing out against the bright green background, ears pricked intently, those fierce yellow eyes watching them with an unblinking stare. Handsome, beautiful even, but terrifying as well, because he had appeared so silently, a wild presence spirited up from the depths of the wood. Stalking them for how long?

'Here, Fang . . . Here, boy . . . Come here, old fellow,' said Peter nervously.

The animal crouched down, as though to spring, and gave a short, sharp bark. Then he turned and melted into the wood.

Mair began to moan. 'I don't like it, Peter. I want to go.'

'We can't till we've got Tar. Do stop being so silly. Look, I tell you what, if you're scared here we'll go to the farm and see if we can find Betsy Tranter and ask her if she knows where he is. He must be something to do with the farm. He kept talking about it and saying "us".'

'That means letting on we've been in the wood. Dad said to steer clear of Mr Tranter.'

'Not if we find Betsy. We can ask her not to say anything to her Dad. It'll be all right so long as we take care not to let anyone but Betsy see us.'

To reach the farm, they had to leave the wood, cross the field again, and take a track which ran from the village to the farm, skirting the edge of the wood. At the village end of the track a cracked signpost pointed to 'World's End Farm'. Underneath was scrawled in white paint 'Keep Out'.

It was a rough track, the surface stony and broken up into pot-holes. For the first hundred yards it was fairly open, running along between two fields. Then, as it reached the side of the wood, it seemed to sink a few feet, with the wood close against it on one side, brambles and undergrowth spilling out here and there through the barbed wire, and on the other side a high bank crowned with a thick hawthorn hedge. It twisted and turned, following the outline of the wood.

Suddenly Peter stopped. 'Listen!' he muttered. 'There's someone ahead. Round the next bend.'

There was a chink of metal on metal, and a scrunch as someone moved his feet about on the stony surface. Then a man's voice, muttering irritably. The feet scrunched again, and an engine fired suddenly, spluttered uncertainly for a few seconds and faded again. The man swore, loudly.

'Someone with a motor-bike,' said Peter. 'A motor-bike that won't go.'

They looked at each other uncertainly.

'We'll go on,' said Peter. 'It can't be Mr Tranter. Farmers don't usually ride motor-bikes.'

They rounded the corner. A scooter was leaning up against the bank, with a young man bending over it, doing something with a spanner. He wore oil-stained blue jeans and a short black leather jacket. As the children approached the engine fired again, and once again puttered into silence. The man cursed again and gave it a kick.

'Morning,' said Peter brightly. It didn't seem much good offering to help. He knew nothing about engines.

The man turned and stared at them for a moment. Then he gave a surly grunt and turned back to the machine. The children walked past him in silence and continued down the track.

'Nice friendly person, I *don't* think,' said Mair.

They continued round a few more bends, then the wood ended abruptly and the ground fell away into a shallow valley, the track continuing between fields of barley towards the cluster of farm buildings crouching in the bowl of lower ground beyond the wood.

'There it is,' said Peter.

Mair began to look anxious. 'D'you think it's going to be all right?'

Peter looked around. 'I can't see anyone,' he said. It was true. Everything was very quiet. Even among the farm

buildings nothing moved. There were only two or three
hundred yards between the outskirts of the wood and the
farm, and there were thorn bushes and snatches of quickset
hedge all along the track. They decided that they could
fairly easily approach the farm unseen, try to find Betsy,
and dodge back to the wood if anyone else appeared.

The farmhouse, a long, low building, was grey-gold stone
like the village houses and stood at the far end of a wide
farmyard, surrounded by barns and cow-byres. It had a
roof of stone slates, bright gold with moss and lichen and
sagging with age so that the ridged outline of the beams
and rafters beneath showed like bones beneath skin. Mair,
always quick to notice things, saw that there was not a
single new building among the complex of sheds and

barns—no shining Dutch barn, or new milking parlour, or brick shed. Everything was old and stone, and slightly crumbling, and had an air of sinking comfortably into the ground. The gate into the farmyard had lost several rungs, and the remaining ones were tied here and there with rope. A cart with shafts—queer sight nowadays—stood outside the barn, and an old wooden bucket with a handle lay on its side by the gate. Ducks and chickens picked their way around the yard, and from the black depths of a shed came the peaceful sound of animals munching.

Outside the farmhouse door lay a dog, fast asleep in the sunshine. An old dog, its coat almost white, but unmistakably a relation of Fang and The Bitch.

There seemed to be nobody about. The children edged cautiously up to the gate and peered through. The dog went on sleeping.

'Betsy must be here somewhere,' said Peter. 'Perhaps if we . . .'

And then the quiet was shattered by a sudden rush of noise behind them. The children ducked down quickly behind a bush, and up the track roared the boy in the jeans and black jacket whom they had seen earlier. He got off at the gate, a small, slightly stooping young man with a thin face and eyes set too close together, threw the machine carelessly down beside the ditch, and climbed over the gate. The bike fell a few feet from where the children were crouched and Mair found herself staring at a pair of crossed flags stencilled on the rear mudguard. The dog woke up with a start and stood up growling: the light caught its eyes and they were the same hard yellow as Goacher's dogs. The man swore at it and it slunk aside. They heard him shout out 'Anyone there?' and, without waiting for an answer, open the door of the house and go in, slamming it behind him.

'He's something to do with the farm, then,' said Peter. Three or four minutes passed and the door opened again and three people came out, the motor-bike man, and an older man and woman, presumably Mr and Mrs Tranter. They were all three in the middle of a furious argument. Their voices, rich with anger, reached the children clearly across the yard.

'. . . If I told you once I told you a hundred times, it ain't no good comin' to me for money, young Luke. I'm not buying you a new one 'o them nasty bikes. I ain't got a penny to spare, and if I had I wouldn't give it to you, nephew or not,' Mr Tranter bawled angrily.

''Twouldn't be right,' Mrs Tranter broke in. ''Tis a waste of good money. Anyways we'll need all we've got put by for Betsy, when she's grown up and thinkin' of getting married, like. You've got your wages at the garage, haven't you? It's all grab with you, Luke, and always was, ever since you was a lad.'

'I always bin ready to take you on at the farm,' said Mr Tranter. 'But no, it was money, money, money with you. Any job so long as it brought in a good wage-packet. I don't understand it—all the Tranters has always been farmers.'

Luke shouted back that he'd be a fool to let himself be stuck away down here working for next to nowt, wouldn't he? And he and Mr Tranter went on scowling and shouting at each other while the chickens stalked unconcernedly around them and the old dog went to sleep again in the sun. The children looked away uncomfortably: they didn't like being in this awkward position of listening to a conversation that was none of their business, but they hadn't much choice. If they got up and went away now they would be seen at once. Betsy Tranter, a stocky ten-year-old with two fat plaits bouncing up and down her back, appeared from round the corner of the house and stood listening. Mrs Tranter, muttering indignantly, vanished into the house again.

At last the argument slackened, and finally stopped, with the two men glaring at each other, both red in the face.

33

Luke turned round and marched off angrily, vaulting over the gate almost on top of where Peter and Mair were crouched. He pulled the bike out of the ditch, started the engine, and roared away again up the track.

'Good-for-nothing!' spluttered Mr Tranter, to Betsy, or the chickens, or nobody in particular. 'Useless young feller he be—spendin' all his time idlin' around. Never done a proper day's work in his life, he ain't. Should be working on the land, not in that mucky garage.'

Betsy sat down on an upturned bucket, chewing the end of a plait, apparently unmoved. The children had the impression that this kind of scene was nothing out of the ordinary.

Mr Tranter strode into a barn, still muttering angrily. There was a terrible roar from within and he emerged driving a very ancient, rusty tractor. The sight of it came as a sudden shock: evidently the Tranters did make some concessions to the twentieth century.

'I be goin' up to Cuckoo Furlong,' bawled Mr Tranter above the noise of the engine. 'Tell your mum, Betsy, there's a good girl.'

Betsy nodded, and set to chewing the other plait.

At the farmyard gate the tractor engine hiccuped a few times, and faded out. Mr Tranter got down from the wheel, gave the side of the machine a violent kick, and it shuddered into life again. Farmer and tractor crawled away up the track.

As soon as he was out of sight the children emerged cautiously from their hiding-place. 'Call her,' whispered Peter. 'Don't go into the yard.'

Mair put her head round the corner of the gate-post. 'Psst!' she hissed. 'Betsy! Betsy Tranter! Come here a minute.'

The old dog opened one eye and growled half-heartedly. Betsy looked up in surprise and wandered over to the gate.

'Hello,' she said amiably. 'You didn't ought to be here,

you know. My dad gets awful cross with strangers coming to the farm. Best not let him see you.'

'I know,' said Mair. 'But we had to. We wanted to ask you something. Do you know the peculiar man who lives in the wood—Goacher? He's got our dog. He was going to mend his hurt paw and he said we should come and get him today but we've been in the wood ages and we simply can't find him. Do you know where he is?'

Betsy's eyes got rounder and rounder all the time Mair was speaking. She stopped biting her plait and let it fall behind her. 'Oh, my goodness! You been in the wood? My dad wouldn't like that at all. And you been talking to Goacher? He don't usually talk to no one, and sometimes he sets the dogs on people. He frightened away those orchid ladies . . . He must have liked you.' She looked considerably impressed.

'He likes Peter, anyway,' said Mair. 'Because he was interested in the hawk.'

Betsy climbed up on the gate and perched on top. 'I know who you are,' she said chattily. 'I like your dad. He's ever so much nicer than the old headmistress we had before. He don't shout at people, and he don't make people put their hands up every time they want to leave the room, and he gives us ever such interesting things to do. We're learning all about those ancient Greeks.' She beamed at them.

'I'm so glad,' said Peter hastily. 'Jolly nice . . . But, Betsy, do you know where this Goacher is? That's what we really came to ask.'

'Oh—Goacher,' said Betsy with less interest. 'He's in the cow-shed—the one round the back. Actually I 'spect that's your dog he's got with him. I saw there was a new one.'

'Oh, good,' breathed Mair.

Betsy slid off the gate. 'Come on. I'll show you.'

'What's he doing in the cow-shed?' said Peter, as they followed her round behind the farm buildings.

'Wart-charming,' said Betsy briefly.

Peter and Mair exchanged mystified looks.

Outside the farmyard, backing onto the house itself and opening onto a field, was another low stone cow-shed, somewhat dilapidated, the roof pock-marked where slates had fallen off. At one side of the doorway, crouched down, nose between paws, but alert and watchful, was one of Goacher's dogs, and, a little further away, sitting contentedly in the sunshine, was Tar.

'Tar!' shrieked Mair, rushing forward. His paw, on inspection, seemed to be healing nicely. There was a brief, ecstatic reunion.

Peter peered into the warm, cow-smelling depths of the shed. There was Goacher, squatted down on his haunches beside a black and white cow, passing his hands back and forth across her udder, mumbling and crooning as he did so.

'*What* did you say he was doing?' Peter whispered to Betsy.

'That old cow's got warts,' she explained cheerfully. 'They often does. Goacher charms 'em away. He's really good at it. Some can and some can't and he's one of them that can. Folk ask him to come and do their cows from all round, but mostly he won't go 'cos he don't like leaving the wood.'

Goacher looked round and saw them. 'You seen the dog? I told you I'd fix 'un, didn't I?' he said with triumph. 'Right as rain, he is now.' He emerged from the shed. Outside, Mair was clutching Tar in her arms, her dark hair streaming down over the dog.

Goacher sidled across to Peter. 'You sure she ain't got the evil eye?' he muttered.

'Not so's you'd notice,' said Peter cheerfully. 'She can be an awful nuisance but not actually *evil*.'

'I heard that!' said Mair, furiously. 'For the last time, I am not a witch. Anyway, there aren't such things. Never were, either.'

36

Goacher looked round anxiously and muttered something under his breath. Even Betsy looked worried. 'You
shouldn't talk like that,' she said. 'It's unlucky.'

'Oh, for heaven's sake, Betsy!' said Peter, laughing. 'I
suppose you believe in ghosts, too?'

'Of course,' said Betsy earnestly. 'My dad's seen one. By
the wood, on a frosty night at Christmas time. No one goes
in the wood at night, 'cept Goacher. But they wouldn't
hurt him, 'cos he's always there and he keeps people out
of the wood.'

Goacher nodded solemnly, his blue eyes glinting from
under the yellow fringe.

'Rubbish,' said Peter impatiently, but Mair, stroking
Tar's short, wiry coat and letting him lick her neck as
much as he liked, for a special treat, thought to herself that
even if you didn't believe in ghosts, there was no denying
that places could have queer sorts of feelings about them.
Maybe you just imagined church bells ringing, and carts
rattling when there weren't any carts, and she certainly
wouldn't care to mention it to anyone, but all the same . . .

'Anyway,' she said quickly, 'thank you very much for
making Tar better. You really are very clever with
animals.'

Goacher smirked.

'Betsy,' said Peter coaxingly, 'do tell me something. Why
is it your dad gets so angry about people going into the
wood?'

Betsy fidgeted and looked intently at her feet. She pulled
her plaits round to the front and began chewing the ends
of both at once in her agitation. Her round cheeks had
gone very pink.

'Orchids,' she said at last, firmly. 'Ever such rare orchids
there are. People might pick them.'

Goacher was listening avidly. 'No, it ain't,' he broke in
with excitement. 'He be afeard folk'll come looking for the
Thing—but I got 'un hidden away and no one knows

where it be and no one'll ever find 'un. It won't never get took away and the sickness won't never come back to Astercote.' He was jigging up and down with enthusiasm, his eyes fixed in a lurid blue squint.

'Goacher!' Betsy turned on him in a rage. 'You shouldn't have said that. They're not village people. Stupid, stupid Goacher!'

Poor Goacher cowered away, mumbling that he didn't mean no harm. 'Him's my friend,' he said, stroking Peter's arm.

'Betsy,' said Peter sternly. 'I don't think you're telling us the truth. What's the big secret?'

'There isn't any secret,' gabbled Betsy, scarlet-faced. 'It's the orchids, honest it is. Some ladies came last year to see them, ladies with walking-sticks and hairy skirts and Dad wouldn't let even them go in though they just wanted to look. So they went round another way and got in—but they didn't stay long.'

'Why not?' said Mair.

'I didn't do nothing,' said Goacher quickly. 'I just looked at 'un from behind trees and made noises. And Fang didn't touch 'un, he just followed 'un.'

'All the same,' said Mair. 'I can quite see why they left in a hurry.'

'I don't believe your father cares tuppence about orchids,' said Peter. 'Come on—tell us. We won't tell anyone else—I swear. What do you mean by looking for *It*, Goacher?'

But Goacher, quelled by Betsy, would say no more.

'All right, sorry,' said Peter. 'None of our business.'

'What's none of your business, young fellow?' said an angry voice behind them. 'And what's your business here, anyways? Who said you could come down here?'

Mr Tranter had appeared round the corner of the shed, without any of them hearing him, and was advancing ominously. He was a big, burly man, very sunburnt and in

38

need of a shave. He wore an unbelievably ancient felt hat, dungarees, and a tweed jacket which seemed made as much of straw as of material, so many bits clung to it. Mair retreated nervously.

'Don't be cross, Dad,' said Betsy persuasively. 'They're Mr Jenkins' children and they didn't mean no harm. They just came to get their dog. Goacher bin looking after it for them.'

'Schoolteacher's children, eh?' said Mr Tranter, his tone becoming more friendly. 'Our Betsy speaks well of your dad. She thinks the world of him.'

'I'm sorry, Mr Tranter,' said Peter, taking his glasses off to polish them on his shirt, trying to hide the awkwardness he felt. 'I'm sorry about going into the wood the other day, but we simply had to find our dog.' There didn't seem much point in trying to hide anything now.

'In the wood, eh?' said Mr Tranter heavily. 'I'm surprised Goacher didn't set the dogs on you.'

'Goacher likes them,' said Betsy eagerly. 'Truly, Dad.'

They turned towards Goacher for confirmation, and suddenly became aware that he and the dogs had vanished, quickly and quietly. A moment or two before they had been there: now they were gone.

'Likes 'em, does he?' said Mr Tranter. 'He don't usually like strangers.'

'Do you mind if we go there again?' said Mair, giving Mr Tranter what she hoped was a melting smile.

He didn't seem the kind of person to be easily melted, but he said again: 'Our Betsy thinks the world of your dad . . . I'm not saying yes and I'm not saying no. Don't you go doing no damage, though.'

'Oh, no,' said the children reassuringly. Mair whistled to Tar, who had wandered off across the field, and they set off to walk home. Betsy came with them a little way, chattering on about this and that. When she had left them Mair said, 'We still don't know who Goacher is.'

'I do,' said Peter. 'At least I think I do. I was looking at him hard this time, and at Betsy, and Mr Tranter, and they've all got something the same about them. Something about their round faces, and their eyes. I think he's Betsy's brother.'

'I don't,' said Mair. 'He says such peculiar things, and pretends not to know about aeroplanes. I never met anyone so odd. I think he's—oh, I don't know what I think.' She stared at the wood in perplexity.

They were half-way along the track now, where it ran close up to the wood, and there was a rustling in the undergrowth. Goacher's head appeared suddenly, framed in the bushes.

'Come,' he said peremptorily. 'I be goin' to show you summat.'

They hesitated. 'Come on,' said Peter. 'Might as well. Find out what all the mystery's about . . .'

They followed him along a tortuous route between the trees, twisting and winding, following a barely defined track through the undergrowth which Peter decided must be a badger path. At last they emerged onto the wide grassy ride through the centre of the wood.

The children looked around. 'What is it we've come to see?' said Peter.

Goacher stopped. 'I be going to show you Astercote church,' he said.

'Astercote?' said Peter doubtfully. 'Where is it? I mean, is it far? Because if it is I think we'd better go there another time. We ought to be going home soon.'

Goacher became suddenly irritable, as though at their stupidity. He waved a hand around and snapped, 'You be *in* Astercote.'

Three

THE CHILDREN looked round them. Before and behind, the green track stretched away through the trees, a wide sunken road, grass-filled, edged with the tall spikes of willow-herb and the luscious, sharp green of spurge plants. And on either side was the wood, a mass of trees in every size and shape, from spindly saplings to massive oaks, the floor carpeted with a tangle of nettle and bramble.

'But this is a wood,' said Mair, frowning. 'Not a village. Astercote sounds like the name of a village.'

Peter had plunged away up the track to investigate something, and now he came hurrying back. 'I say,' he said, 'I thought it was funny there being so many stones around and the way they looked kind of arranged. Well, there's a sort of wall there—or what's once been one. Goacher—were there houses here once?'

'I told you this be Astercote. Houses be all around you —church be further up. You want to see 'un?'

And now they began to see that the shoulders of stone beside the track must mark the cottages, and the grassy mounds and hillocks the places where other walls, all but crumbled away, lay hidden under the ground. The trees had grown up above and around, and if you hadn't been told it would have been difficult to see what suddenly became so obvious.

'Why did the houses fall down?' said Peter with interest.

The reply was incoherent: something about many winters ago, after the sickness, when the people had all died.

'Oh!' said Mair suddenly. 'Do you think he means the Black Death? You know—whenever it was that thousands of people died?' She looked round, and shivered. The wood seemed colder, all of a sudden.

'Must be,' said Peter. 'Whatever it was, it was obviously ages and ages ago. There's practically nothing left. What about this church, Goacher?'

Goacher led them further up the track, and after a minute or two stopped. At first they saw nothing: the track had narrowed a little, and a huge oak tree spreading across it cut off the light. And then, staring confusedly at the side of the track, they began to see the stones. Worn, tumbled stones, cloaked with ivy and brambles, but nevertheless, recognisably the remains of walls. Here and there a sapling had seeded itself right among the stones and pushed them further apart as it grew, and fingers of ivy probed every crevice and held the bigger stones in a smothering embrace. And there was one slender, fluted column, ending in the broken-off curve of what was unmistakably the point of a gothic window.

'I say!' said Peter excitedly 'He's right. There has been a church here.'

Exploring among the stones, they found traces of a paved floor under the grass and brambles. Goacher circled round them anxiously, admonishing them not to touch anything. It was clear that he felt some kind of guardianship for the church, but at the same time he was highly pleased by their interest and kept pointing out more stones, and slabs of paving, and another fluted column, fallen onto its side and half-buried in the undergrowth.

Mair sat down on it and looked about her. At Peter, scrabbling about under the leaves to look at the stones, at the dogs, Fang and The Bitch, squatting on their haunches, silent and watchful, never taking their eyes off their master, at Goacher himself, with his tawny thatch of hair and brown, weather-worn limbs. She looked up, and the green

42

of the leaves overhead pulsated with blinding flashes of light, the whole mass moving and swaying, the sunlight snapping down through it, flashing and dazzling. Mair stared until she began to feel dizzy and had to blink and turn away, her heart throbbing. She shook her head sharply and tried to focus on Peter, still burrowing away in the undergrowth, and a queer sensation took hold of her. As on that evening coming across the field, she again had a dream-like impression of some other world, a different notch in time, with people going about their business . . . Bare feet shuffling on a stone-flagged floor, someone chanting, high and monotonous, chickens scratching in the dust, things moving, talking, animals, people . . . The tang of wood-smoke, a smell of dung and warm straw . . . Then Peter said something, and the feeling went away.

'I've just thought,' she said, 'Goacher—this is where you got the font from, isn't it, that the dogs were drinking out of?'

An ugly flush crept up Goacher's neck and spread across his face. 'I didn't mean no harm,' he said guiltily. 'I weren't going to spoil 'un. I didn't think no one would mind. And I always kept watch on the Thing.' His voice dropped, and he eyed them speculatively, as though about to make some suggestion.

'Oh, I'm sure no one minds,' said Mair hastily. 'I mean, who'd be likely to, anyway? Does anyone else even know about the church?'

But Goacher didn't answer. He was still mumbling about how he'd meant no harm, and it were safe with him, and no one would ever find 'un . . . It didn't make much sense. However, his first suspicions of them seemed to have changed completely to an attitude of acceptance, even enthusiasm. He kept plucking at their arms to attract their attention, show them this and that, gabbling on in his strange, thick speech. He was like a child, Mair thought, who assumes that you know all about its life and never

44

troubles to explain what it is talking about. And the dogs, sensing his trust, had dropped their reserve and would allow themselves to be stroked, nudging the children's hands with their great heads.

Suddenly Goacher said, 'I be goin' to show you summat else—summat I ain't never showed no one before.'

'We really ought to go,' said Peter doubtfully. 'We've been gone ages. We'll come back tomorrow.'

'No! No!' cried Goacher. He was dancing up and down now, the thick yellow fringe bouncing against his forehead. 'I be goin' to show you the Thing. There ain't many as has ever see'd it—not since they all died and it were hid so the sickness wouldn't never come back.'

There was something in his voice, an urgency and an intent, that silenced the children. Peter hesitated, and looked at Mair. Mair, torn between curiosity and apprehension, felt a tiny shiver trickle down her back.

'All right,' said Peter at last. 'Which way?'

Goacher led them deep into the wood, twisting and turning so often that soon they had lost all sense of direction. The wood was full of noise and activity: wood-pigeons crashing in the branches overhead, the alarm call of a jay, tracking them from somewhere above their heads, the rush and whisper of leaves. Mair looked up, and again there was that mesmerising flash and sparkle of sunlight through the branches. She looked firmly away: for some reason she found she did not want to be Mair-in-the-past just at that moment

At last Goacher stopped in a small clearing, dominated at one side by the huge trunk of a very old oak tree. He peered round apprehensively, and then, his eyes blazing with excitement, squatted down and began scrabbling with his hands at a large patch of loose soil and leaf-mould at the foot of the tree, in a triangle formed by its spreading roots.

'Wait,' he said. 'I be goin' to dig 'un up for you.'

'What on earth!' said Peter. 'Dig what up, for goodness' sake?'

Mair took several paces backwards. 'I don't like it, Peter,' she said, in a high, tight voice. 'I'm scared. I'm not going to look.'

'Don't be daft,' said Peter. 'It'll be something quite ordinary.' But he was very still, staring with fascination at Goacher's stubby, brown hands scraping away the soil.

Mair shut her eyes. 'Tell me when he's finished,' she said in a small voice.

They were all silent, even the dogs. At last Goacher sat back and beckoned to Peter. 'Come and look,' he said, 'I can take 'un out now.'

Peter stepped forward and looked over Goacher's shoulder. 'It's all right, Mair,' he said in a relieved voice. 'You can look. It's just a bit of old sacking with something wrapped up in it. What is it, Goacher?'

With clumsy care, Goacher was unwrapping the folds of the sacking, still laid on the brown earth.

'Gosh!' said Peter, as the last fold was pulled aside. 'A sort of cup. What on earth . . . ? I say, do look, Mair.'

They bent over it. It was a dull yellow colour, tarnished here and there, with a glint of silver in places. The bowl was wide and shallow, supported by a stem eight or nine inches high, on a hexagonal base. Half-way up the stem the metal swelled out into a circle of tiny, carved heads barely half an inch wide, and the children, looking closely at them, saw that they were the same round, fringed faces as the gargoyles on the church in Charlton Underwood. On one facet of the base there was a crude engraving of the crucifixion against a background of squares and diamonds roughly scratched on the metal, and the figure on the cross had the same round, wide-eyed, thatched face. There was a feeling about the cup of loving care, as though whoever made it had known that he was not making a thing of great beauty, but something that reflected what he knew, simple, direct and uncomplicated.

46

'It's a chalice,' said Mair, in an awed tone. 'Like you see in churches. Standing on the altar.'

'It's very old, isn't it, Goacher?' said Peter, gently touching the little heads with a finger. 'Very, very old. Thank you for letting us see it.'

'I suppose,' said Mair slowly, 'I suppose it's been here ever since they died and the houses fell down. It's gold, isn't it? But how do you know about it, Goacher?'

Goacher was babbling almost uncontrollably. Piecing together what he said they began to make sense of the story. After the last of the villagers had died someone—someone whom Goacher could not name but sometimes referred to confusingly as 'us' or 'we'—had taken the chalice from the church and hidden it. Hidden it because it belonged to Astercote and in Astercote it should remain. And because, or so they began to understand from Goacher's vague, confused talk, because whoever took it had come to believe that it enshrined something precious, something magical, that would prevent such a catastrophe ever happening again.

'The sickness won't never come back,' he kept repeating. 'Won't never come back to Astercote, nor to Charlton. Not so long as we got 'un safe—the Thing—so long as it stays in Astercote.'

'But, Goacher,' said Peter in a matter-of-fact voice, 'it wouldn't come back anyway. People don't get the plague any more. It was all to do with rats, and bad sanitation and things. It's been quite stamped out now.'

Goacher looked at him blankly. ''Twon't come back so long as we keeps 'un safe here,' he repeated.

'Do other people in the village know about it?' said Mair. 'In Charlton Underwood, I mean?'

Goacher's answer was, as usual, devious, but he seemed to be trying to say that people knew of its existence, and of the importance of it never being removed, but not exactly where it was.

47

'Only you know?'

'We allus knew at the farm. Us at the farm allus took care of 'un and kept 'un hidden,' said Goacher proudly.

'I don't know,' said Peter doubtfully, turning the chalice over and over in his hands. 'I'm sure it's terribly special and ought to be in a museum or somewhere.'

Goacher leapt up in extreme agitation. 'You won't take 'un! You won't tell where I hidden 'un!'

'No, no, of course not,' said Mair soothingly. 'Don't be an idiot, Peter. Can't you see how much it matters to him? Of course no one's going to take it, Goacher, and we won't breathe a word to anyone at all. Not even our mum and dad.'

They watched Goacher wrap the chalice reverently in the sacking and re-bury it, carefully scattering leaves and sticks over the place. Then they hurried away, and much later Mair, in the silence and blackness of the night, dreamed that the chalice hung like a great golden moon over the pointed spire of a church buried in swaying trees, while all around hunched figures with gargoyle faces came and went, and came and went.

The wood became a kind of magnet. They found themselves making for it almost every time they left the house, across the field, ridged like a great sheet of green corrugated paper, past the cows, and up the gentle slope to the wood, rippling and shifting in the wind, silent, brooding, guarding its secret, older than the fields, and the houses, and the road.

Goacher had come to accept them completely, though it was always Peter that he favoured, clutching his arm and squinting up at him for approval, gabbling on about the animals and the wood and his strange, peaceful life. He was totally absorbed in the wood and never left it except to go to the farm for food, or for shelter if the weather got too bad.

48

'Do you never go to the village, Goacher?' said Mair curiously, but he shook his head, mumbling something about people staring at 'un.

'I be goin' to fly old bird,' he said. 'D'you want to come and see 'un?'

'You bet!' said Peter enthusiastically.

Goacher had the hawk on his wrist, the great hoops of its claws dug deep into the thick leather gauntlet he wore, in fact a motor-cyclist's glove. It was tethered by the feet with a leather thong which was in turn attached to a short leash, the end of which Goacher held between two fingers. The glove, Mair saw with distaste, was deeply stained with dried blood.

Peter moved towards it eagerly, and at once the bird stiffened, half-spread its wings and collapsed backwards off Goacher's wrist, fluttering and kicking with a total loss of dignity, like some panic-stricken hen. It hung upside down, struggling, for a minute or so until Goacher persuaded it back onto its perch.

'Shouldn't never come up at a hawk like that,' he said reprovingly. 'It makes 'un bate.'

'Sorry,' said Peter. The bird, still ruffled, turned its head away, the fierce eye glaring, a mad, offended gaze.

'And don't stare at 'un,' Goacher added. 'You shouldn't never look a hawk in the eye. He thinks you be goin' to attack 'un.'

They followed Goacher at a respectful distance, out of the wood, across the track and then through a gap in the hedge into a grassy field dotted here and there with thorn bushes and sloping away at the far side up to a steep bank under a hedge. The bank was scarred all over with the brown traces of rabbit burrows. Goacher stopped and the dogs moved up to him expectantly.

Mair clutched Tar tightly. He was, after all, not much bigger than a rabbit and that bird looked thoroughly dangerous, she had decided.

Goacher snapped an order to the dogs and at once they sloped off towards the far end of the field, one each side, encircling the bank, running low to the ground, heads down. The hawk had roused, and seemed to be watching. Peter saw Goacher slip the leash from between his fingers.

Fang was half-way down the field now, keeping close to the hedge. And then, so suddenly that it was impossible to see where it had come from, there was something brown swerving across the grass in front of him in a frantic, crazied dash towards the burrows. Goacher shouted, and the dog pulled back, and in the same moment Goacher swung his arm back and sent the bird hurtling forward, the leash trailing from the great yellow feet. For a moment it seemed to hang uncertainly, and then it was going up, up with a great spread of wings, and down below the rabbit was zig-zagging desperately over the grass, nearer and nearer to the burrows.

"E won't get 'un,' said Goacher angrily. "E be goin' to stoop too late.'

The hawk, still climbing, seemed to struggle against some invisible force that sought to press it back to the ground, and then it turned at the crest of its climb, magnificently mastering the air, the sky, the whole world, and for a split second hung, a great, malevolent shape against the sky, and then it was plummeting down, dropping through the air as though it were a great weight, so fast that they could hear the rush of the wind through its feathers. Mair clapped a hand to her mouth to stifle a yell of excitement.

Down, down—and then there was a flurry on the ground, and the bird was crouched over the limp brown rag of the dead rabbit. It allowed Goacher to come up to it, take the rabbit and substitute a gobbet of meat from a pouch at his belt. Evidently the rabbit was for Goacher's dinner, not the hawk's.

'Ugh!' said Mair, turning her head away. 'Beastly.'

50

Goacher flew the hawk once or twice more, unsuccessfully. The rabbits succeeded in escaping to burrows or the hedge and the bird, after flapping around disconsolately returned on its own accord to Goacher's wrist.

'I don't suppose he'd go to anyone else, would he?' said Peter with envy. 'I mean, it's just you he knows.'

Goacher snorted. 'He don't know nobody, old bird. 'E be right stupid—they all be, hawks. 'Tis the glove 'e knows. You trains 'em to the glove. Then 'e only has to see 'un and 'e'll come back to 'un every time.' The bird sat crouched on his wrist, tearing delicately at a lump of raw meat with its curved beak.

'Come on,' said Mair, getting up from the grass hummock she had been sitting on.

'I've had enough. It's nearly dinner-time. Let's go.' She felt slightly nauseated.

'I bet it's stew, Mair. All lumps of meat. Bits of animal. Rabbit stew, probably.'

'Shut up,' said Mair coldly. 'Anyway, it's fish fingers. I know because Mum said.'

Goacher was not a person who went in for formal goodbyes or arrangements to meet again. He was already shambling off into the wood as though he had forgotten their existence, the hawk on his wrist and the dogs at his heels. A man and his animals, with the grass below and the sky above: a united, timeless group, as much a part of the landscape as the group of elms on the hill spreading their graceful, irregular outlines against the horizon, and the black scatter of rooks circling round them.

'I wonder if you can fly hawks at rooks,' said Peter thoughtfully, with a sideways glance at Mair. 'Rook pie . . .'

'Stop being so bloodthirsty and come on.'

At the point where the track joined the lane through the village a small car was standing, precariously tilted sideways, one wheel lying on the ground beside it. A girl in a blue dress was heaving another wheel out of the back of

51

the car. She looked up as the children approached, pushing her hair out of her eyes with an oil-stained hand. The blue dress, Mair saw, was clamped neatly round her waist by a wide black belt fastened with a silver buckle, and there were crisp white cuffs to each sleeve above the elbow.

'Can I help?' said Peter.

'Thanks,' said the girl. 'I wasn't going to do the damsel in distress stuff—seeing as how I'm quite capable of changing a wheel myself—but that jack's jolly stiff and my arm aches.' She plumped herself down on the grass, stretching out black-stockinged legs in front of her.

'Where we lived in Wales,' Mair said, 'Dad always used to say if you saw the nurse it meant a coming or a going.'

'A birth or a death. I like that—it couldn't be anything but Welsh. Well, it's the same here, I suppose. It was a coming this morning. Mrs Knight at the pub. Another daughter. Come from Wales, have you? Oh, you'll be Mr Jenkins' children, then?'

Mair nodded. 'I'm Mair. He's Peter.'

'And I'm Evadne Fletcher.' She laughed. 'Did you ever hear such a name! And for a district nurse, too.'

She had dark hair, almost black, crisp and curly, and very dark brown eyes, sharp and interested. She looked foreign, almost, Mair thought—Italian or something, but she spoke just like other people in the village. She must have been about twenty-five. Mair, suddenly aware that she had been staring, turned her head away in embarrassment.

Evadne Fletcher laughed again. 'I know—you're thinking that district nurses ought to be fat and fifty, with arms like bolsters. Well, I daresay I will be one day, when I've been at this game a bit longer. My mum used to do it, you know, and she looked the part a bit more, but she wanted to retire and put her feet up, poor old love, and I'd just qualified so I took over last year.'

Peter tightened the last bolt on the wheel and put down

52

the spanner. 'I hope that'll do,' he said. 'I've only done this once before.'

'Don't worry,' said the nurse. 'I daresay it'll be all right and if I find myself spinning along on three wheels I'll know who to complain to, won't I?'

Peter sat down on the grass beside them. 'Have you always lived in the village, Miss Fletcher?'

'Look, love, if you don't call me Evadne you'll be the only person in the village who doesn't. Yes, since the year one—born and bred. Real old Charlton type, I am. Mum too. Though when she was the nurse the County hadn't got around to dishing out cars—it was bicycle for her, wet or fine, winter or summer, and on foot when the snow came. She's got lots of stories—dashing off to deliver babies on Christmas Eve in the snow and all that sort of thing. Once she had to go down the track you've just come up, to the farm, and the snow was so deep she had to wade through the drifts almost up to her waist. She thought she'd never get there.'

'To the farm?' said Mair sharply. 'To the Tranters . . . ?'

'That's it. Mrs Tranter was expecting her first, and Mr Tranter came up to say she'd started and would Mum come, and they struggled down there through the snow together, with those dogs slipping in and out of the trees, and not a sound anywhere. Eerie, it must have been.'

'And the baby?' said Mair with interest.

'Oh, it came all right. A boy, it was. Poor little chap.' Evadne sighed.

'Why, what happened to him?'

'Nothing, then. But later, when he was older, he had a very bad illness, and it affected the brain. There wasn't anything the hospital could do. They sent him home when he was better, but they had to tell the Tranters he'd never grow up any more mentally, as it were. A dreadful tragedy for them.'

There was a silence. Evadne got a comb out of her bag

53

and began to tug it through her hair, using the car bumper as a mirror.

'They've got Betsy now,' said Mair at last.

'Mmmn. Good thing she's a sensible kid or she'd be as spoilt as they come. They're a funny pair—the Tranters. Like to keep themselves to themselves. There's been Tranters at World's End since the beginning of time: they're even said to be the same family as cleared the land in the first place, hundreds of years ago, but I don't know about that . . . And they're the old kind of farming people, not business-men driving tractors like you get nowadays. Very rooted. Very touchy about the land. Bit too much so, perhaps—but there you are, they can't help how they're made.' She bent down to smooth a wrinkle out of her stocking and put on the shoes she had kicked off. 'I say, I don't know what I'm doing sitting here nattering like this. Oddly enough they pay me to do this job.'

'I'm not being rude,' said Mair, 'but you don't look a bit like most of the people in the village.'

'Ah!' said Evadne, and laughed again. 'Me flashing black eyes, you mean. That's Sergeant Joe Corelli of the United States Air Force, that is.'

The children gaped.

'My dad,' said Evadne. 'My dad was an American pilot— at Brize Norton during the war. Came to a social in the Village Hall, and swept dear old Mum off her feet.' She giggled. 'Seems funny to think of now—twelve stone without her shoes she is—but she was young and sylph-like then . . . Anyway, love at first sight it was, and they got married, and Mum was expecting me, and the war ended and Sergeant Joe Corelli went off home to his dear old home-town in Arkansas to get things ready for Mum and me to come, and then one Saturday night he went out on a binge and had a lot to drink and crash, bang! Into a lamp-post with the car on the way home and that was that.'

Mair was shocked. 'You mean he was killed?' she said

disapprovingly. This didn't seem any way to talk of one's father's death.

'Oh dear, now you think I'm a heartless brute, don't you? But honestly, I never even met him, so to speak—and it's all such a long time ago.'

'But your mum?'

'Oh, Mum . . . She had a good weep, and then she up and married Tom Fletcher from over the road who she'd known all her life, and had Billy, and Maureen, and Colin, and we all lived happily ever after.' Evadne smiled sweetly. 'Me swarthy complexion, and a wild name like Evadne—that's all we've got to remember the Sergeant by.'

'Oh,' said Mair, confused, 'I see.'

'Do you like Charlton Underwood?' said Evadne, moving towards the car. 'Too much of a backwater for you? Or do you like the country?'

'I'll say we do,' said Peter enthusiastically. 'It's been jolly good so far.'

'People speak well of your dad. Mind, I've not come across many people from the new estate yet myself—they tend to dash off to hospital to have their babies and that, not like the old village people.'

'I love it,' said Mair. 'The wood specially. I didn't at first —I thought it was creepy. Now I like it—though it still gives me a funny feeling sometimes.' She spoke vaguely, almost to herself.

Evadne gave her an interested look. 'Does it indeed? Well, I really do have to go. Thanks ever so, Peter—I hate changing wheels.' She climbed into the car and the children watched her drive away down the road towards the old village.

'That was good,' said Peter. 'Changing the wheel. It's just a question of getting it jacked up right, and then bashing on with the spanner. *Now* perhaps Dad will let me do it on our car next time we get a puncture. You will tell him I did it, won't you, Mair? I mean, don't be too

55

obvious about it, just mention it casually. Mair, for goodness sake *listen!*'

'Mmmm? Sorry, I was thinking . . . Oh, yes, but you'll have to remind me. She was nice, wasn't she? You heard all that about him—about Goacher?'

'Yes,' said Peter, frowning. 'I suppose the wood, and the lost village and everything has sort of got more important to him than the real world, so he just ignores things outside, and things he doesn't understand like aeroplanes, and pretends they don't exist. Mad, really—but not dangerous mad. I guessed all along it was something like that.'

'I didn't,' said Mair rashly. 'Do you know—I even thought once, after he first showed us the church and everything, I even thought he was left over from when it all happened.'

'That, you great nut, would have made him about six hundred years old.'

'I know,' said Mair dreamily. 'But I still thought it for a bit.'

'Typical. Absolutely typical. Have you ever noticed that people don't actually live to be six hundred years old? In fact most of them pop off before they're one hundred. How many people over a hundred do you know?'

'I'm not telling you. And that's the last time I'll ever tell you anything I've thought. You always laugh.'

'All right. Don't get in a temper about it. You must admit it was a dotty idea.'

Mair had been collecting a handful of burrs and decided to end the conversation by stuffing them down Peter's shirt.

'Oh, all right, then!' he spluttered. 'If that's the way you want it . . . Come on, Tar, let's get her!'

He stooped and caught her foot, tripping her up and sending her rolling into a culvert choked with meadowsweet and grasses, and throwing himself after her. They thrashed about in a spray of pollen and grass-seeds, with Tar circling round and round, yapping hysterically, uncertain who to protect from whom, until Mair shrieked that something crawly had got inside her shirt and she'd had enough. She insisted on stripping to her vest and pants while Peter hunted for whatever it was.

'A ladybird. Just about dead with fright anyway. Honestly, Mair! Do get your things on—someone might come. If you could only see yourself . . .'

'I'm the girl in that art book at school, with no clothes on and flowers in her hair. Flora, or whatever she's called.' She began prancing about, twisting strands of creamy meadowsweet into her tangled hair. 'Venus coming out of the sea . . .'

'An advert for washing powder, more like. "Persil will get your daughter's vest as white as this." Only you're all covered with grass stains. Mum's going to be thrilled. I'm off, and if someone comes along and sees you like that, you're nothing to do with me, got it?'

At some point in the depths of the night Mair was woken by Tar whining in the kitchen downstairs. She was the only one to hear him, partly because her room was above the kitchen and partly because, childish as it might seem, she still liked to leave her door open at night for that reassuring crack of light from the landing. Still dizzy with sleep, she swung her legs over the edge of the bed, paddled around the mat for her slippers, couldn't find them, and stumbled barefoot down the stairs. Tar was squatted by the back door, his stubby tail batting about impatiently as he watched her come. Dad must've forgotten to let him out last thing, she thought blearily, anyway, at least he hasn't made a puddle. She fumbled with the locks and got the door open at last. Tar trotted briskly out.

Mair leaned against the door-frame, shivering slightly as the night air stroked her bare arms, slowly waking up. Come on, Tar, get on with it, I want to get back to bed. It was almost light, with a strange, flat, toneless light that puzzled her until she realised that there must be a full moon lurking somewhere, hidden behind trees or houses. Looking towards the old village, she saw the jumbled houses, and the church tower, the fine stone gleaming pale, almost white, against the other blacks and greys of trees, road, bushes and grass. It was a world drained of colour, very still, everything somehow larger and more majestic than by day. The church might have been a cathedral, the houses grander, even older. A bat swept past only a few feet away from her, its tiny body sharp against the sky, black against black. Mair yawned, and looked round for Tar.

He was sitting at the end of the garden, where nothing but a low fence separated them from the fields and she realised with surprise, not having noticed before, that you could see the dark mass of the wood from there. She took a few steps forward to call him in, and the moon swung into view, a flat yellow disc above the trees, colour at last in this black and white night world. She stared at it, and as she stared it seemed to pulsate, no longer a hard circle but ebbing and flowing at the edges like some primitive jelly-creature seen under a microscope. And didn't it have black specks all over it now, and weren't there yellow streaks shooting out from the edges . . . ? She blinked, and shifted her gaze to the soft black spread of the wood below. Wasn't there something about moonlight making you mad? It was all very beautiful, though, everything swimming in this queer, milky light: she felt she could stand there for ever, watching and listening.

Tar was very alert and intent, sitting squarely on his haunches without moving, still looking towards the wood. And then his back hairs stood up in a dark ridge, and Mair felt a prickling in her scalp, as a low, sobbing howl drifted over the fields, quiet at first, and then reaching up to a peak, and then dying away again, and then starting up once more, over and over, for fully a minute. That's Fang, thought Mair, or the other one. What a creepy noise—I'm glad I'm not in the wood now. She almost turned to look back at the house for reassurance, and then didn't, because the dreamy, detached feeling that she could now recognise had come back—the sensation of being no longer Mair now, but Mair then, a watcher Mair in some other time, passive recipient of sounds and smells that were real, and yet unreal . . . And this time, she found with surprise, feelings. Sensations were washing over her, of cold, and fear, and hunger, and then suddenly, relief. A man was walking, under the moon, through snow, and he was listening to the same sobbing howls, only now they came from all round, nearer, and then further again, and he was so tired, and cold, and then he looked towards the place where the wood should be and there, under the same high, swinging moon, he saw the pointing finger of the church spire, Astercote spire, and everything was all right. A jumble of silver-washed thatched roofs, and the black shape of the church, and somewhere the round orange glow of a lantern, and the cold, and the exhaustion, began to recede. Someone, sometime, a long while ago, came home late at night when the snow was piled against the hedges and in the forest there were howlings . . .

Mair felt something warm against her leg, and looked down to see Tar gently nosing her feet. Her arms were very cold, and she could hardly feel her toes at all. The moon had vanished behind a cloud, the garden had darkened, the wood was just a silent black mass against the dark sky and that pencil-shape standing out was just a tree taller than the others, not a spire lifted above houses.

She picked Tar up and went back into the warmth of the kitchen.

Four

BETSY WAS in the wood, head down among the spurge and bracken at the side of the wide track, eating wild strawberries.

'Hello, Betsy,' said Peter. 'Mind you don't tread on any of those orchids you were telling us about.'

Betsy's round face bobbed up, pink with heat or embarrassment.

'Don't take any notice of him,' said Mair. 'He's only teasing you. Can I have a strawberry?'

'They've mostly gone,' said Betsy. 'I always forgets about them till they get all squashy and the birds have ate most of them. But you can have these—if I eat any more I'll get a tummy-ache.' She held out a cupped hand, grubby and berry-stained.

'I come looking for Goacher really,' she said. 'They was a bit bothered because we haven't seen him for a day or two, and The Bitch was hanging around the farm by herself. Usually he has the dogs with him. You seen him?'

'Not today,' said Peter. 'And we weren't up here yesterday or the day before.'

'Never mind,' said Betsy vaguely. 'He'll turn up, like as not.' She sat down on the grass beside Mair, staring with unabashed admiration.

'I think you're ever so pretty,' she said after a few moments.

Mair felt awkward. She didn't know how to deal with that kind of remark, even from someone as unassuming as Betsy. Not, come to that, that it was a remark that people made all that often. She was glad Peter was out of earshot or he'd have been getting at her about it for days.

'And your dad's ever so clever,' Betsy went on with enthusiasm. 'He knows about *everything*.'

That was easier. 'Not absolutely everything,' said Mair, feeling that truth was more important than loyalty. 'But a lot about things he's specially interested in. History—at least particular bits of history—and poetry.'

Betsy nodded wisely.

From further up the path Peter called out that he was going home. Mair got up to follow him. ' 'Bye, Betsy,' she said kindly. 'See you . . .'

Betsy's normally cheerful face drooped with disappointment. 'Oh,' she said, and then, with a flash of inspiration, 'would you like to come to tea? At the farm?'

'What, now?' said Mair doubtfully.

'Yes,' said Betsy, wriggling with excitement. 'Mum made bread this morning so there's lots to eat.'

'Well, I don't know really. I mean, your mum might not like it. Us coming just like that. Usually we'd ask our mum if it was all right, or your mum would ring her up and ask if we could come, and all that sort of thing.'

61

'Oh,' said Betsy humbly. 'I didn't know. I never asked anyone to tea before.'

Mair melted. 'I'm *sorry*, Betsy. I'm stupid. Of course we'd love to come to tea—if you really think your mum won't mind.'

Betsy led the way chattering happily. At the entrance to the farmyard Mair and Peter stopped and looked at each other.

'Look, Betsy,' said Mair, 'don't you think you'd better go in first and ask your mother if it's all right? We'll wait here.'

They stood in the sunny farmyard. Flies buzzed round a heap of manure in one corner. Sparrows popped in and out of cracks among the lichen-covered slates of the roof. Chickens wandered around them, lifting fastidious feet. The big white dog they had seen before stood up on long, spindly legs and stared at them before lying down again in a different position.

Betsy appeared again in the darkness of the doorway, beckoning, and they followed her in, still a little apprehensive.

They found themselves in a large kitchen, quite different from the antiseptic whiteness of most of the kitchens they knew. The floor was stone-flagged, the stones rubbed smooth to a shining patina of merging reds, browns and greys. There was a strong, not entirely pleasant smell from a side of bacon pinned to the great beam in the centre of the ceiling. A huge, scrubbed table, uncompromisingly plain, dominated most of the room. A vast brown dresser against one wall housed plates of every size and pattern, as well as being festooned with cups and jugs slung from hooks, an ancient felt hat, a canvas bag, a pair of sheep-shears, a very rusty rifle, and a selection of enormous keys that looked more appropriate to the Tower of London. There was a couple of comfortable-looking, but very dilapidated basket chairs, a tattered calendar for 1948 hanging from a hook over the sink, and another dog, an ordinary sheepdog this time, lying sprawled under the table. Mrs Tranter was standing in front of an old black stove, doing something to it with a poker.

She turned as they came in, and they saw that she had Betsy's round face and blue eyes. There was an awkward silence, and Mair thought, how funny, she doesn't know what to say either, I didn't know that happened to grown-ups as well. Betsy looked from one to the other of them expectantly.

At last Mrs Tranter said, a bit sharply: 'Well, sit down then, while I put the kettle on. You'll have to take us as you find us, I'm afraid. We don't have many visitors down here.'

'Shall I butter bread or something?' said Mair. 'I do at home.'

Mrs Tranter seemed to relax a little. Both the bread and the butter were home-made. Mair cut and spread, savouring the rich, yeasty smell. Betsy watched, glowing with pride. Her happiness seemed to communicate itself to her mother, whose first awkwardness was rapidly disappearing. By the time they sat down round the table they were all talking quite naturally.

'Like it all right, in the village, do you?' said Mrs Tranter. 'Living in one of them new houses, I suppose?'

'Mmm,' said Peter, his mouth full of delicious, coarse bread. He remembered his father saying that not all the old villagers had taken kindly to the coming of the new estate and added hastily: 'I expect you feel it spoils the village a bit, all the new building.'

'I don't know,' said Mrs Tranter vaguely. 'I don't go up to the village above once a month or so, anyway. Our Betsy brings me back my bit of shopping and most of what we need we've got on the place.'

'Mum don't come from Charlton Underwood,' said Betsy, with the air of one explaining an important fact.

'No,' said Mrs Tranter, 'I'm not from these parts. Only come here when I married George—but that's a long time ago now.'

'Where was your home, then?' said Mair.

'Long Barton, my dear,' said Mrs Tranter. 'More bread? You look as though you could do with feeding up a bit.'

Peter and Mair stared at her in surprise. Long Barton was barely three miles away. Goodness, thought Mair, Wales might as well be Timbuctoo, at that rate.

Mrs Tranter plied them with food. Come here often and we'd be as fat as old Betsy, thought Peter. He grinned at Betsy and she beamed back sunnily.

Presently Mr Tranter came in. At first he seemed put out to see them, and the atmosphere of diffidence and mistrust which had met them when first they came into the kitchen returned, but after a while, mellowed perhaps by Betsy's chatter, he began to relax and even to join in the conversation.

Peter asked about the dog outside. 'Is she a relation of Fang and—of the ones in the wood?'

Mr Tranter hesitated a moment and looked away quickly, busying himself with spreading jam on an enormous hunk of bread. 'Yes,' he said, 'that's right. She's the Old One. Reckon she won't do much longer, the old lady, she's near blind now and she don't get about much. By the way, The Bitch been hanging around again—did you find Goacher, Betsy?'

Betsy shook her head and Mr Tranter looked faintly troubled.

'Poor thing,' said Mair. 'Still, she looks happy enough, just lying about in the sun.'

'They're awfully odd dogs, if you don't mind my saying so,' said Peter. 'Sort of Alsatians gone wrong . . . They have such long legs, and funny eyes.'

And they howl like—like I don't know what, thought Mair.

64

'They be good watch-dogs,' said Mr Tranter shortly. 'And we always had 'em here at World's End. My dad had 'em and his dad before that and long before then.'

'Isn't it bad for them to keep—er—marrying each other? In the same family, I mean,' said Mair, and then blushed.

'Inbred?' said Mr Tranter. 'That what you mean? Could be, I suppose. Sometimes we mates the bitches to a sheep-dog. We only keeps a pup when it looks a good, strong 'un, anyway.'

They did not enquire what happened to the others.

After tea there was a general bustle of activity. Betsy was despatched to the field to bring in the cows and the children watched them file slowly into the long, low cow-shed where the cobbled floor was worn almost smooth by hundreds of years of shuffling feet. As Mr Tranter moved about among the swishing tails and heaving flanks, crashing milk-churns against the floor, Peter realised with mild astonishment that the Tranters still milked by hand. There were no machines. Daringly, he asked if Mr Tranter had ever thought of installing one.

'Temperamental things,' said Mr Tranter briefly, dismissing the march of progress. 'Go wrong more often than they works properly, and then where are you? Back where you started, with a bucket and your two hands. Anyway,' he added as an afterthought, 'we haven't got the electric down here yet, and not likely to neither.'

They wandered around the farm buildings with Betsy on a kind of conducted tour. They smelt the lovely pungent smell of apples in the apple-store, watched Betsy chivvy an indignant hen that had insisted on laying her eggs in the hedge, looked at the potato clamp, and the pig-styes, and the great, cool barn where a stone mill-wheel stood in one corner.

Peter pointed to it. 'Does your Dad still use that?'

' 'Course not,' said Betsy scornfully. 'Corn all goes away in sacks now. But I think Grandad did, or maybe his dad.'

The sun was beginning to sink in the sky now, but the stones of the buildings, apricot in the evening light, breathed out the heat they had been absorbing all day so that Mair, leaning up against the wall of the barn, felt it soft and warm all up her spine. All the noises of the farm were muted and blurred, like the late afternoon light: the chuckle of the chickens, rumbling of a woodpigeon somewhere among the trees, occasional thumpings from Mrs Tranter working in the kitchen. They said goodbye and set off for home. Mrs Tranter came to the door, her hands flour-speckled.

'Tell Goacher to come down here if you see him on the way back, will you? That dog was wandering around the place howling like a lost soul all last night: he'll have to tie her up.'

They heard the dog themselves from the path by the wood, the sound coming muffled from somewhere deep among the trees. Tar fretted, anxious to go and investigate.

'Do you think there's something wrong with it?' said Mair.

'Goacher'd see to it if there was, wouldn't he?'

But it disturbed them, and finally, just before the bend where the track left the side of the wood and pointed across the fields to the village, they decided to go into the wood. For the first ten minutes they called Goacher, expecting his round, squinting face to appear suddenly from the undergrowth, but there was nothing to be seen or heard, except the occasional howl of the dog, the sound distorted by the trees so that, thinking that it came from the clearing, they followed it there, to find it empty except for the hawk. It had been raining hard that day and the wood was still and sodden, the trees dripping and the leaves squelching under their feet. The hawk was on its perch, its head sunk almost into its feathers, half-asleep, looking damp and dejected. But there was no sign of Goacher, nor yet by the ruined church, where they searched among the silent stones and the brambles. They had not heard the dog for a while now, but then, just as they were thinking of going home, it started up again, with a low, throbbing howl, nearer now.

'It's this way,' said Mair, plunging off through a stand of purple willow-herb. Peter followed her, wincing as a trail of bramble wrapped itself round his leg. Looking down, he saw beads of blood strung out across his calf.

It was a damp, stinging and scratching progress through pathless undergrowth, but they could hear the dog quite clearly now, whimpering and whining.

'We've been here before,' said Peter suddenly. 'We're getting to the place where he showed us the chalice. Look —you can see the big oak sticking up above the others.'

A few minutes later they were in sight of the big tree. The dog was standing beside it. She looked thin, as though she had not eaten for several days, the ridges of her ribs clearly visible under her coat. When she saw them she growled, but her tail swung to and fro, and in a moment the growl gave way to a whine, and the pricked ears flattened.

'Here, Bitch,' said Peter, holding out his hand. 'Come here, old girl. What's wrong, then?'

But the dog did not move. She stood quite still, staring at them expectantly.

'Peter!' said Mair suddenly. 'Look!' She was pointing at the place between the spread roots of the tree where Goacher had shown them the chalice. The covering of dead leaves had been scattered, and freshly turned earth, sticky wet from the rain, was spread around. A few feet away lay the piece of sacking, as though flung down in a hurry.

For the next few minutes they searched feverishly. Then Peter said in a puzzled voice, 'It's gone. The chalice. He's taken it away.'

'Or someone else has,' said Mair anxiously.

'No. It must have been him. He said no one else knew it was here. He must have wanted to put it somewhere else.'

'But why? And where is he? And where's Fang?'

They looked around in bewilderment. An owl screeched somewhere in the trees, making Tar dive under a bush in panic. It was getting very dark.

Mair was stroking The Bitch. 'Poor old thing . . . Where's Goacher gone, then?'

'Well, she can't tell you, can she?' said Peter impatiently. The branches above their heads were rustling and stirring as heavy drops of rain began to fall.

'Come on, we'll have to go or we'll get soaked. We haven't got our anoraks.'

Mair got up reluctantly. 'I don't like leaving her. And I wish we'd found Goacher.'

'Oh, she'll be all right—after all she always lives in the wood. Presumably he'll come back. The Tranters weren't all that worried. Come on—it's going to thunder.'

The sky above the clearing was almost purple, like a rich dark bruise, and everything was very still. There were no bird-noises. Mair didn't like thunderstorms. 'All right,' she said hurriedly, 'we can come back tomorrow, perhaps.'

They hurried away, stumbling and crashing through the trees until they found the path again and could run freely to the edge of the wood and wriggle out through the barbed wire and into the field. The gathering storm was behind them now, right above the wood, and the trees, standing out clear and bright against it, had taken on a strange, fierce intensity of colour, vibrant green against the mass of slate-dark cloud pressing down upon them. As they watched white light exploded across the sky.

'Here it comes!' said Peter, and even before he had finished speaking the thunder crashed over their heads.

And as the rumble died away to the edges of the lowering sky Mair heard the bells ringing in the wood, clearer and louder than she had ever heard them before, the sound floating across the fields in the silence of the approaching storm. The bells of Astercote, ringing and ringing, up and down the scale . . . Ringing for a mass, or for the end of the day, to call in the cowherds . . . Or ringing for a death, or for a warning . . . ? She stared, transfixed, at the green trees, and the grey bellies of the clouds above, until the rain was falling heavily on her hair and bare arms, and Peter was calling back at her to hurry up or she'd get soaked, and then the thunder crashed again and when the noise died away the bells had stopped ringing and there was just the steady patter of the rain and the soft swish of cars on the road.

Five

'IT'S FOUR DAYS we ain't seen him now, near enough,' said Mr Tranter, taking an unbelievably large bite out of a cheese sandwich. 'Reckon he must be sulkin' about summat, hidden away somewhere. He can be awkward at times, poor old chap.'

The children had come upon the farmer by chance, eating his dinner by a hedge. A field of ripe barley seethed all around them, the ears rattling and clicking in the wind.

'Start harvestin' next week,' said Mr Tranter absently, 'if the weather holds.' Betsy was lying on her stomach beside him, pulling burrs out of the sheepdog's coat.

Peter and Mair looked at each other, questioningly. They had not been back to the wood since the evening they found the chalice missing, but the whole affair had disturbed them. They'd not talked of it, but Mair knew that Peter had been thinking about it too, from the way he'd kept lapsing into thoughtful silences, and the very fact that he'd not suggested going there.

Something had to be said. Peter took a deep breath and said it.

'Mr Tranter. We went to the wood to look for Goacher the day before yesterday, and we couldn't find him. But there was something funny . . .'

'Eh?' said the farmer sharply.

'Well—please don't be angry about it—but before that, just a few days ago, Goacher showed us what's hidden in the wood. What he calls the Thing. I don't expect he should have—but he just wanted to be friendly, and of course we'd never tell anyone, or touch it or anything. Well, anyway, when we went to look for him we went back to the place where it was because the dog was howling there—and—and, well, it had gone.'

'Gone?' the farmer turned round angrily, and Betsy looked up, her round face solemn and scared. 'What do you mean, gone.'

'Someone had dug it up,' said Peter helplessly. 'There was just a hole. We thought perhaps Goacher had decided to move it somewhere else. Thought it wasn't safe or something.'

Mr Tranter was on his feet. 'You come along with me,' he said grimly, gripping Peter's shoulder. 'I'm havin' a look for myself.'

They made their way through the wood, Mr Tranter in front, still gripping Peter's arm, and Mair and Betsy hurrying behind. Nobody said a word, Peter, despite his alarm, noticed that Mr Tranter made straight for the big oak tree: clearly he knew where to go.

The Bitch was still there. Mair was relieved to see some rabbit bones near by: evidently she had got herself something to eat.

And so was the bare, turned earth and the piece of sacking. The farmer turned it over with his foot, ond poked around among the leaves. Betsy drew close to Mair, looking very anxious.

And then Mr Tranter began striding up and down the clearing like a man possessed, pushing The Bitch aside impatiently as she nosed his leg, ignoring the children, searching among the leaves on the ground, parting the bushes, slashing at nettles with a stick. They watched him in frightened silence.

At last he stopped, muttering to himself distractedly. 'It's gone,' they heard him say. 'It's gone. This shouldn't never have happened. We shouldn't 'a let Goacher mind it. He weren't fit.'

71

'Mr Tranter,' said Peter nervously, 'if it was really valuable—oughtn't you to ask the police to help find it? I mean, they could find Goacher and then if he's got it everything would be all right.'

The farmer turned on him angrily. 'This be our business,' he snapped, 'and nowt to do with anyone else. We don't want no police around the farm. If Goacher took it then Goacher'll have to put it back. I been creditin' him with too much sense—shouldn't never a' trusted him with it.'

Mair said suddenly, 'Could someone have stolen it?'

'In that case, then why's Goacher disappeared?' said Peter, with more confidence. 'Anyway, I thought he'd never shown it to anyone before us.'

'He did. He did once,' said Betsy, in a small, frightened voice, but nobody heard her. She went over to The Bitch and buried her face in the dog's warm fur.

Mr Tranter stopped pacing up and down and stood in front of Peter, thrusting his angry face forward. 'And don't you be giving me no advice, young fellow. This be none o' your business. Goacher had no right showing it to you, for that matter. How do I know you ain't got summat to do with it going?'

'Dad!' said Betsy in a shocked voice.

Peter and Mair looked at each other, stricken. Then Mair said indignantly: 'We wouldn't even have *thought* of touching it. Or telling anyone where it was. You shouldn't have said that.'

The farmer sat down on a log, as though overcome with exhaustion. 'I'm sorry. I don't rightly think you touched it. It's the shock, see.' They saw that his hands were shaking.

I'd better shut up, thought Peter, I seem to say the wrong thing all the time.

'I 'spect it'll turn up,' said Mair comfortingly. 'I mean, if Goacher took it then when he turns up again he'll bring it back, won't he?'

'It certainly better come back, and come back quick,' said the man. 'It bin here always: this is its place. Could be a terrible thing for us if it really be gone.'

Oh no! thought Peter in astonishment. He believes it too—the story about the Black Death. I thought it was just Goacher, because he's a bit funny in the head. But ordinary grown-up people! It seemed like believing in the tiger under the bed, or the witch behind the door. He'd laughed at Mair once and made her cry, years ago, when he'd found out she had to look under the bed every night before she got into it. And his father had been angry with him and said 'Don't you be so superior about it, boy. She's not such a freak. There's plenty of grown-up Mairs around, I can tell you. It's easy to know in one part of your mind that a thing's not possible, while the rest of you's screaming out that it's real, and you're scared stiff.'

And suppose you were Mr Tranter, and had lived in this one place very uneventfully all your life, not bothered about much except your cows, and the weather, and the family, and this story of old Astercote which you'd always known but didn't talk about much? And then the thing you'd always been told mustn't happen, happened? Perhaps it wasn't all that astonishing.

'Come on, Mair,' he said abruptly. 'I think we'd better go.'

Mair was silent until they were out of the wood. Then she said in an off-hand voice: 'It really is true you don't get the plague nowadays, isn't it?'

'Oh, for heaven's sake! Not you too . . . No, you *don't*—not since the eighteenth century or something, or at least only in India and places like that. You really are daft, Mair.'

'I read a book once . . . It was horrible, people just dropping down dead in the street, and once they'd got it they knew they were almost bound to die. Sometimes it began just with sneezing—Ring a ring 'o roses, pocket full of

73

posies, tishoo, tishoo, all fall down—that came from the plague. All fall down dead, you see.' She shivered. 'And once someone in a family had got it they shut them all in the house and chalked a great cross on the door and there they had to stay—and at nights carts came and took away the bodies to great pits to be buried. And there were disgusting descriptions of what it was like—the illness, I mean —they got great swellings under their arms and all over that turned into sort of boils . . .'

'Do you mind?' said Peter. 'We'll be having dinner before long.'

'And sometimes the people who'd got it went mad and danced about the streets until they dropped. The Dance of Death.'

'Just as well it's been stamped out, then,' said Peter cheerfully. 'Sounds nasty.'

'Poor Mr Tranter—and Betsy. They were awfully worried.'

'It'll be all right. Goacher'll turn up and it'll all have been a lot of fuss and bother about nothing.'

'I hope so,' said Mair. 'I do hope so.'

Next morning, their first thought was to get down to the farm to find out if Goacher had appeared. But it was raining at breakfast, a heavy determined rain that flattened the flowers in the garden and kicked up a fine spray from the pavement outside, and they had to wait until the clouds began to lift before they could set off. They walked through the new estate, across the main road that separated it from the old village, and past the church, to reach the track leading to the farm. They took the short cut through the churchyard and Mair, looking up, saw the round, ugly faces of the gargoyles scowling down at her below the gutter, and was reminded of the tiny heads on the chalice. The gargoyles stared back, stony-eyed, and she thought, with a flicker of wonder, that they must have been doing that, rain and shine, summer and winter, since before the people of Astercote had died, and the other church had fallen down, and the wood had grown up over it.

'That was what happened,' she said aloud. 'Wasn't it? The wood grew up over the village, not the other way round. After it was deserted.'

'Mmmm,' said Peter. 'Dad says it's called a lost medieval village. It was just the forest taking over again—the sort of forest that covered England nearly all over before people started carving chunks out of it to make into fields. Oh— and you know how the fields by the wood are all lumpy, with ridges up and down them? Well, that's left over from when they were ploughed up in the old days. They were the big open fields round the village and everybody had a strip to grow things on. Mair, you're not listening.'

'I am,' said Mair abstractedly. She had turned to stare back at the honey-coloured huddle of the old village beyond the church. Astercote must have been a bit like that, she thought. More thatch, probably. And lots of mud buildings as well as the stone ones. And a track instead of the road. And the bones of it are still here, under the countryside as it is now, the stones, and the lumps in the wood, and the shadows on the field when the light is right. And the people still knowing about it at the back of their minds, even though they've got televisions and washing-machines like everywhere else. And poor Goacher, all mixed up about who he is so that he feels safer in Astercote than anywhere else. And me, hearing bells and things. Perhaps I'm getting mixed up too?

They were nearly at the corner of the track now, where the signpost pointed to World's End Farm, and Peter began to walk on impatiently thinking: she can jolly well run and catch up if she won't even listen when I'm saying something interesting. Just as he reached the corner there was a scrunch of tyres on the loose surface and a car came out and turned onto the main road. It was Evadne's. Peter thought, with a stir of curiosity, that she couldn't have been anywhere but the farm.

The farm was very quiet in the windless, grey morning. The cows were out in the field behind the barn, mostly lying still or standing motionless, like a child's cardboard cut-outs on a model farm. The dogs were silent, and there was no noise of tractor, cart or milk-churn. The only activity was the house-martins dipping and swerving over the roofs and the farmyard, sometimes settling in chattering rows on Mrs Tranter's clothes-line.

Getting ready to migrate, Peter thought. I ought to take notes, every year, about how early I first see them doing that, and where, and for how long, and all that kind of thing.

Mair, looking at them strung out along the line like beads in a necklace, thought: they go to Africa, don't they? To deserts and jungles and places, and look at quite different things, and then come back here, the same birds, and look at the farm, and the wood, and us. How very odd . . .

They hung around for a while behind the farmyard wall, hoping that someone would come out and enable them to size up the situation without actually having to take the step of knocking on the kitchen door.

'Maybe they're out,' said Peter, after nearly ten minutes.

'Don't be silly. They never go out.'

'We'll have to knock. It's silly to go away without—now we've come down here.'

They crossed the farmyard. There was no bell to the door, but a heavy, rusty iron knocker which filled the whole place with an embarrassingly loud noise when Peter lifted it and let it fall again. Chickens rushed, gabbling, for the safety of the barn, and the sheepdog came flying from somewhere behind the house, barking furiously. They stood, awkward, waiting for something to happen.

For several minutes nothing did. The chickens subsided and the dog sat down in the mud, watching them.

76

And then an upstairs window was flung open and Mrs Tranter looked out.

'Hello,' said Mair, taking a step backwards to see her better, 'I hope you weren't busy. We just wondered if—if Betsy'd like to come out with us.'

'Go away,' said Mrs Tranter quietly. 'Don't ask no questions, just go away, quick as you can . . .'

It was like a slap on the face. They stared up at the window, too astonished to speak.

'I told you to go,' she said again, in a strange, harsh voice. 'Go quickly—don't come no nearer—and don't come back here again.'

Peter touched Mair's arm. 'Come on,' he said quietly.

They walked quickly away across the yard. At the gate Mair turned once to look back, but Mrs Tranter had gone. The windows were black, empty, and everything was still again, except for the martins looping and swerving against the grey of the stone roof.

They didn't say anything until they were almost back to the village. At last Mair said: 'But why? *Why* . . . ? I mean, what have we *done*? I thought they liked us.'

'So did I. Betsy did, I'm sure, and Goacher . . .'

'It's something to do with the chalice. They must still think we took it. Oh—how *could* they!'

'I'm not sure it's that,' said Peter slowly. 'It was peculiar, but she didn't say go away in a really angry voice. More desperate . . . Don't you think?'

But Mair didn't answer, lost in indignation.

At the end of the track Peter stopped. He had seen Evadne's car parked outside a cottage.

'Wait a minute. I want to ask her something when she comes out.'

Mair, still wallowing in hurt feelings, didn't answer, and they stood by the car until Evadne came out of the cottage a few minutes later.

'Hullo, you two,' she said. 'That tyre's still on, by the way.'

'Evadne,' said Peter, 'I saw you come back from the farm this morning. From the Tranters. Is there something wrong there?'

'Mrs Tranter was ever so—well, rude,' said Mair. 'It wasn't a bit like her.'

Evadne paused, half in the car, and then stepped out again. 'I shouldn't worry about it too much,' she said after a moment, hesitantly. 'I told you they were a bit—well, a bit old-fashioned. They've got something on their minds just now.'

'We know,' said Peter. 'About the chalice. Goacher showed it to us. And it was us who found it was gone and told Mr Tranter.'

Evadne looked surprised. 'Oh,' she said. 'Oh, I see.'

'But it was different today,' Mair persisted. 'I mean, she told us to go away—just like that. I thought they were friendly to us.'

'Is there something else wrong?' said Peter.

'Well, in a way,' said Evadne. She seemed worried, and reluctant to tell them more. 'Betsy's got mumps,' she said at last.

'Mumps!' said Mair, on the verge of laughter. 'Is that all! Did she think we might get it? Anyway, we've both had it.'

Evadne was silent.

'Is she very ill, then?' said Peter. 'Mumps isn't usually serious, is it?'

'No . . . No, she isn't really very ill.'

'I daresay she feels miserable,' said Mair with sympathy. 'I remember when I had it. You get horrible swellings behind your ears and places.'

Horrible swellings . . . Lumps . . . Even as she said it, and saw Evadne looking closely at her, she began to realise something.

'They do know it's mumps, don't they?' said Peter anxiously.

'I told them,' said Evadne. 'I told them again and again.'

'But they don't believe you . . .' said Mair. 'That's it, isn't it? They don't believe you. They think it's the Black Death.'

Six

'COULDN'T THE doctor come?' said Peter. 'Surely they'd believe him? I mean to say,' he went on confusedly, 'maybe they might feel the doctor was more—well, more serious. If they're rather used to you—feel you're just part of the village.'

'They won't have a doctor near the place, not now nor any other time. Got no time for doctors, Mr Tranter hasn't. Not after the business with Goacher.'

'Well,' said Mair, 'she'll be better in a few days, won't she? And then they'll realise it wasn't. It'll have been a lot of worry for nothing.'

Evadne was silent. She began to stow her black bag away on the back seat of the car in a careless, distracted way, frowning to herself.

'She will be better in a few days, won't she?' said Mair.

Evadne climbed into the driving-seat and wound the window down so that she could answer. 'Look, love,' she said, 'when people are ill, how quickly they get better depends a lot on their state of mind, as well as on the illness itself. It's what they teach you in hospital nowadays when you're training: it's supposed to be all very modern but really it's as old as the hills. Mum knew that just as well as I do. Stands to reason—if you know there's nothing very serious wrong with you, you recover a great deal quicker than if you convince yourself you're going to die. See?'

The children nodded.

'And Betsy thinks, and her parents think, that she's very ill indeed. And nothing I say—and believe me I've been saying and saying all morning till I'm blue in the face— will make them think otherwise. And it's not doing old Betsy any good.'

'She won't die . . . ?' said Mair fearfully.

'No, but she may not get better all that quick, either. And there's another thing . . .'

'What?'

'I don't know what's going to happen when it gets round the village that she's ill.' Evadne sat drumming her fingers on the steering-wheel, staring straight ahead of her.

'You mean there might be a sort of panic?' said Peter, a tinge of excitement in his voice. 'Other people might believe—what the Tranters believe? Hysteria,' he added knowingly.

'Oh, I don't know,' said Evadne, 'but they're funny people in the village, some of them, and I should know. I've been with them most of my life. Believe in anything, some of them would. And it's got around—about the old cup being pinched. Lot of tutting and head-shaking there was in the pub, our Billy said, among the old folk. Anyway, don't say anything to anyone about Betsy and maybe it'll all blow over.' She started the engine. 'I'll be down at the farm again in the morning to see how Betsy's getting along. Drop in at my place around dinner-time and I'll let you know how things are.'

They went home past the church and Mair, looking up at the gargoyles, thought that their stone grimaces had changed to grins of malice.

In the morning the grey lid of cloud had lifted, giving way to a streaming mist through which a weak sun shone, promising a fine day later. The grass in the garden was frosted over with a thick dew, so that Tar's footprints were like a pattern of black pennies. The children left the house early, and wandered through the estate, past the neat, un-fenced front gardens, whose owners had already established an identity for themselves with rows of standard roses, like enormous Victorian posies on sticks, or rampant nasturtiums, trailing uncontrolled over paths and pavement, or restrained beds of lobelia and alyssum. Windows opened and tousled mop-heads appeared, dustbin lids clattered, children called to one another and rang bicycle bells, a milk-float purred along beside the kerb. Everything was discreetly busy, and normal.

They passed the church, and the school, where the sun flashed on the panes of the modern, glass-fronted building. The main road, running past the new housing estate, separated it from the church and school and the row of cottages beside them, and a small lane running down beside the church widened out to become the village green, with the pond at one end and the houses of the old village overlooking it all round. This was the centre of the old Charlton Underwood: a few lanes and alleys ran down from the green to other cottages, but no road led out of it at the far side, and the lane by the church was the only access to the main road.

Peter and Mair strolled round the pond. Some small

boys were fishing for tiddlers at one end, with more hope than expectation, and some ducks cruised around in the middle. A lorry was delivering crates at the pub, and a boy on a bicycle, whistling, pushed newspapers through cottage doors. The post office and shop had just opened, and somebody came out to give the window a polish with a duster.

All quite ordinary. A morning like any other.

Aimlessly, they walked back to the main road and along in the direction of the track that led down to the Tranters' farm. Mair noticed that the blackberries in the hedge were ripening, and there was a brief scuffle when Tar tried to follow up an interesting smell by the roadside.

It was Peter who saw it first. He had been walking a few paces ahead and reached the corner of the track before Mair did. It sent a cold shiver down his back.

Right in the middle of the notice that said 'World's End Farm' someone had chalked a white cross. Big and bold, almost obscuring the lettering.

Mair caught up with him and he pointed, silently. They stood side by side, staring at it.

'In the real Black Death they used to put them on the doors,' said Mair. 'I suppose this was the closest they could go—or wanted to. How horrible.'

'It's crazy. Absolutely daft. Nobody in their right mind could believe . . . But it's like Evadne said. And it means other people must know already. Well, anyway, it's not our fault; we didn't tell anyone.'

'Do you know?' said Mair, half to herself, 'I think I know how they feel. I could feel like that too if I'd lived here all my life, right by the wood.'

' Oh, come on, Mair! You'll be saying next *you* think it's the Black Death.'

'No,' said Mair hastily, 'I don't. Because I believe Evadne. She's so sensible.'

' " Both feet on the ground and no nonsense," like Mum says.'

Just before dinner they went to Evadne's cottage, a tiny two-roomed affair at the far end of the green. She was eating a cold pork pie in the kitchen.

'Come in, come in. I'm just off really. I'm rushed off my feet—twelve visits this morning and I don't know how many more this afternoon. A baby on the way in, and old Mrs Case on the way out, I'm afraid; and all the rest are the other thing. I'm almost out of my mind, I can tell you.' She didn't look it, though, a compact, competent little person, efficiently tidying away the remains of her dinner as she talked.

'The other thing?' said Peter. 'We saw the cross on the sign. Who did it?'

Evadne shrugged. 'Goodness knows. Might have been any one of a dozen or so I can think of. They've got the wind up all right. I was nearly three quarters of an hour with Mrs Leacock, trying to convince her that her Sandra's sneezing is no more than a cold in the head. There's always someone with a cold in that family, and nobody ever took a blind bit of notice before. And there's three more cases of mumps—but you just try telling them it's mumps. And Miss Barton by the church complaining of mysterious aches and pains, and there's not a thing wrong with her, far as I can see.'

'How's Betsy?' said Mair.

'Not too good. They're in a right pickle down there: Mr Tranter hadn't even got himself out to milk the cows until I just about shoved him out with me bare hands. But we can't go on like this: I've rung through to the doctor and asked him to come out tomorrow and try to make them see a bit of sense. They won't listen to me, any of them.'

Evadne finished getting herself ready to go out again and they walked to her car with her. Tar had run off to bark at the ducks on the pond and Peter went to catch him.

'I'm glad we met you,' said Mair. 'If we hadn't I think

I'd have felt scarey too about all this. There's a funny feeling about this place sometimes, and the wood specially.'

'Oh,' said Evadne casually. 'The bells, I suppose you mean.'

Mair stared at her. 'Do you hear them?' she said in astonishment.

'Not now. But I used to years ago when I was younger. About your age, I suppose—no, younger I think.'

'Don't you ever hear them now?'

'No, duckie, not for years. I'm too busy thinking about what calls I've got to make today, and not to forget the baby clinic at three, and old Mr Lay's injection this evening, and all that kind of thing. You have to be in the right state of mind to hear them. Kind of open, receiving things from all directions, not thinking too much—dreaming in the daytime, not knowing if it's Monday or Tuesday, or morning or afternoon . . . That really only happens when you're a kid.'

Mair was silent. She felt both reassured and at the same time faintly affronted that her experience should be shared. At last she said: 'Peter doesn't hear them.'

'No, he wouldn't. He's one of those busy-minded folk. Nothing wrong with it—just a different type. My brothers didn't either.'

'They were awfully loud the other day,' said Mair, 'as though they knew something was wrong . . .'

'Now, now,' said Evadne cheerfully, 'let's not get too mystical, shall we? I've got work to do and you've got to go home for your dinner before your mum gets after you.'

There was bright sunshine that afternoon. Several times the children caught sight of Evadne, popping about the village on foot and in her car, but she did not notice them, her brown face screwed up in concentration. Several times they passed small groups of people standing talking, but when they came near the conversation died away until they had passed. Once Mair stopped to give a small child a toy that it had thrown out of its pram, and at once the mother came running out of her cottage and swept the child away inside without a word. They could sense a strange atmosphere of brooding, and waiting. Two strangers in a car, visiting the church, were met with surly silence when they asked where they could buy a postcard, and went away, perplexed. Mrs Jenkins, buying bread and bacon at the village shop, was surprised to find the usually garrulous Susie behind the counter sharp and uncommunicative.

But the children played around the green as they always did, and in the evening the motor-bike brigade, the leather-jacketed boys of the village, gathered round the big oak by the pub as usual, lounging, revving their engines, and finally disappeared all together with an ear-shattering roar in the direction of the main road. Mr Jenkins, though, coming home after an hour or so in the pub, complained that he hadn't been able to get anyone to say two words to him.

'Did it matter, Dad?' said Peter slyly. Their father's loquaciousness was well known: he could talk for ten or fifteen minutes on end, pausing only to take a breath.

'That'll be enough from you, boy. Anyway even a Welshman can't talk to the air, can he?'

'Funny,' said Mrs Jenkins, 'they've been quite friendly up till now to us from the estate—the people in the old village, I mean. Perhaps somebody said something to offend them.'

After that Mr Jenkins settled down to a long disquisition about traditional values not being changed by things like television and cars in places like Charlton Underwood, to which nobody said anything very much except Mrs Jenkins, who, from natural politeness and long use, said 'Yes, dear,' and 'Is that really so?' every time he seemed about to stop. Mair thought her own thoughts and Peter, trying to follow a western on the television with the sound turned off, found to his surprise that it was very easy, and decided always to do so in the future.

The first thing they saw when they went out the next morning was the doctor's car, large, expensive, and black, sliding round the corner past the church and down onto the green. It stopped outside Evadne's cottage and the doctor, young and brisk in a new-looking tweed suit, got out and walked quickly up to the door.

All around the green, curtains twitched, and then fell back into place.

Three minutes later the doctor and Evadne came out together and drove away in the doctor's car.

Three hours later Mair and Peter were sitting in the sun on the grass verge outside Evadne's cottage, waiting for her to come home for dinner so that they could ask how Betsy was. They had been there for about half an hour: Evadne was late. During that time there had been plenty to watch. A travelling salesman, with a suitcase of brushes, had parked his car in front of the pub and made a tour of the neighbouring houses. He had had thirteen doors closed firmly in his face, one after the other, and finally drove away disconsolately. A group of women had stood talking in a doorway for a long time, in low voices. Two cyclists in yellow capes had called at the shop and asked for ice-creams, and were turned away, told that a new delivery was awaited, though only five minutes before a little girl had come out eating a cornet. A middle-aged couple in a car had arrived, and walked slowly around, exclaiming in quiet voices about how delightful, and quite unspoilt, it all was. They had gone into the pub, cheerful and expectant, but came out half a minute later, saying to each other in surprised voices that it had *looked* open and surely all pubs opened in the middle of the day?

There didn't seem to be much of a welcome for strangers in Charlton Underwood that morning.

At last Evadne came home.

'What a morning!' she exploded, half amused, half despairing. 'Never in all my life . . . ! They're behaving like people possessed. I can't do a thing with them.'

'What did the doctor say?' said Peter.

'He started out laughing when I told him what it was all about—and I could just see what he was thinking behind that smooth face of his: silly little country bumpkin nurse, with her wild story about village superstitions and crazy ideas. "Soon get it sorted out," he said. "Just a few firm words, nurse, that's all it needs." And I could see he thought I'd brought him out here for nothing. So down to the Tranters we went first, and do you know what—old Tranter wouldn't let him in the place! Said he'd take the shot-gun to him if he put a foot inside the door.'

'He never . . . !'

'He did too. And the doctor was grumbling away about crazy back-of-the-woods farmers, but a bit amused too. Thought it was going to make a jolly funny story to tell his friends, I daresay. And then he said, well, if the child's only got mumps and you say there are no complications, I daresay they can do without me and in any case the man's got a legal right to refuse me entry if he wants to, and where do we go next? Still thought it was all a bit of a joke, he did. So then we went to the Leacocks, and he had a look at all the children and told Mrs Leacock a bit sharpish there was nothing wrong with any of them except colds in the head, and Mrs Leacock just looked at him, blank, and he could see she didn't believe a word of it. And then we went to Miss Barton, and it was the same thing there. "Touch of fibrositis," he told her. "Keep warm and rest a day or two and you'll be as right as rain." And the old dear sat there glaring at him and mumbling because she'd not got her teeth in, and it was just as well he didn't catch what she was saying . . .'

'Why? What did she?'

'Said he was a daft young fool and he didn't know nowt.

88

And then we went to one or two more, and each time it was the same. Sometimes they listened to him and smiled and nodded and said yes, and any fool could have told they were just going on thinking what they thought before; and other times they didn't even bother to listen. He was getting a bit fed up by then, I can tell you, but interested too in a superior sort of way. "Interesting example of self-induced hysteria," he kept saying. "Rather unusual. I believe there was an instance somewhere in the west country some years ago. Might be worth looking at a bit more closely—do a little article for the Medical Journal."

'That kind of thing. But not really talking to me—s'pose he thought I was too dim to understand long words and all that. So we saw them all, and then I said: "What treatment do you suggest, Doctor?" Very efficient and business-like, or so I hoped. That threw him for a moment: he couldn't think of anything at first, and then he gave me a whole lot of chat about creating a calm and rational atmosphere, and things like this being rather out of his field, and letting things run their course until they snapped out of it. And I said: "But, Doctor, these people are frightened." And he said, yes, it was a bit of a problem, but he had this meeting at the hospital and he'd have to dash or he'd be late, and off he went.'

They were in the kitchen, Evadne cutting herself sandwiches off a loaf of bread and hunting around for something to put in them.

'Worst of it is,' she said, 'I'm beginning to think I'm the only one keeping my head. Even mum—my mum, who had a hospital training and should know better—even Mum's started whispering in corners, with the women. I could strangle her. Only people who're taking no notice are the young ones—the teenagers—too busy with their bikes and their dances on Saturday nights. And a good thing too. It's the old folk are the worst—they started it all. Honest, I feel torn in two, I don't mind telling you: one half of me wants to give them all a good shake and tell them to pull themselves together, and then when someone from outside like the doctor comes and is all uppish and patronising, then I'm on their side and I want to say: "I know, dearie, I understand, I was born here too, I know the story . . ." ' She slapped a dried-up slice of ham onto the bread and began to eat it irritably.

'I don't know why I'm telling you all this,' she said suddenly. 'After all, you're only kids. Anyway, there's no need for you to get all bothered about it too.'

'There is,' said Mair, offended. 'The Tranters are our friends. Or were . . .'

'Sorry,' said Evadne. 'Sorry, sorry. Oh dear, what a storm in a tea-cup—or storm in a chalice, I suppose I should say. What a fuss over a bit of an old thing like that.'

'It was very special,' said Peter, 'queer-looking, and beautifully made.'

'I wouldn't know,' said Evadne, her mouth full of ham sandwich, 'I never saw it.'

'Has anyone in the village seen it?' said Peter.

Evadne looked taken aback. 'Well, come to think of it— I don't know that anyone ever has. It was just supposed to be *there*—supposed to have been there always—but no one wanted to know more than that. There was a business when I was a kid when some of the boys got talking about it one night and said they were going to go and find it for a lark—and off they went with spades and torches, but Mr Tranter came out and set the dogs on them and back they came pretty quick.'

'Then we might be the only people who've ever seen it,' said Mair, 'us and Goacher.' She was silent: the thought was somehow impressive.

It was Peter who said, 'Which makes it unlikely that anyone from outside would ever believe that it even existed.'

In the morning the crosses had appeared. There were three of them, on the doors of three different cottages, and another, huge, scraped on the rough surface of the church wall beside the lane leading down to the green.

'It's a joke,' said Peter, staring at it. 'Someone's done it for a giggle—the motor-bike boys, most likely.'

But somehow neither of them believed it.

Two other things had happened. The village shop had closed its shutters and put up a notice announcing that it was closed for its annual staff holiday, though the house-wives from the new estate, frustrated as they wheeled their prams down to the green to get bread and groceries, told each other indignantly that the old villagers were still being served through the back door. And outside the rented cottage next to the pub a furniture van appeared. The people who had rented it for the summer, a young couple from Birmingham, said evasively that they were obliged to cut short their stay owing to a sudden family crisis. They were gone by dinner-time, leaving an over-flowing dustbin on the step and an old mattress, which somehow found its way into the pond where it served as a target for stones thrown by small boys.

And there was something else. In the local paper, tucked away among the football results and Women's Institute activities, was an item headed 'Superstition in a Midland village.' Peter read it carefully and then handed it to Mair.

'Here, look at this.'

'In the tiny village of Charlton Underwood,' she read, 'local people are disturbed by persistent rumours of a mysterious illness. Not many people in the village were willing to talk to our reporter but he did manage to un-earth a curious old legend connected with the Black Death of 1349 which de-populated the neighbouring village of Astercote, now vanished without trace.'

'Rubbish!' said Peter. 'It hasn't vanished.'

'I know. It doesn't say anything about the chalice. They wouldn't have told him about that, I suppose. I don't like

91

the way it says "As readers will know, bubonic plague is now unknown in European countries." Poking fun at the village people . . .' She threw the paper down in disgust.

Later that day came the first sightseers. It took Peter and Mair, wandering in the bright September sunshine, some time to realise that there were more people around than usual, and that not all of them came from either the old village or the new estate. There was a gaggle of girls on bikes who hung around the green for a while, and stared at the crosses, whispering, before they rode away again. And a few middle-aged women got off the bus, waddled around a bit, and then went away on the next bus. And later, as the shadow of the church spire lengthened and stretched itself across the village pond, and the swallows looped and dipped around the eaves of the cottages, the cars began to come. Not many—just one or two at a time. They'd drive slowly round the green, staring out at the houses, and maybe stop for a moment before they went away again. Once Mair saw a fat woman with tight-curled hair point to one of the crosses and laugh, and the man with her laughed, and then they drove away.

'They shouldn't laugh!' she cried in sudden fury. 'It isn't funny. They shouldn't come spying . . .' It's like people who stop and stare at car accidents, she thought.

It was the people in the shiny new Ford who started the trouble, or Tom Craddock, difficult to say which, really. The people had parked their car between the pond and the pub, carelessly, almost blocking the road, and had got out and were lounging about, a man and two women, staring at the houses and laughing a bit. Tom Craddock came down past the church for his evening pint at the pub, a big, tough farmer, said to be a relative of the Tranters. When he was still some way away the man said something to the two women and they both giggled. When Tom got near them he stopped.

'Were you looking for summat?' he said slowly.

'No,' said the man, very casual. 'Just having a look round. Nice place here. Heard you'd been having a bit of trouble, though?'

Tom Craddock didn't say anything, but he took his pipe out of his mouth and stuck it in the pocket of his jacket. Mair, watching from outside Evadne's cottage, hoped it wasn't hot enough to burn a hole. Her father'd done that once.

'Don't know about no trouble,' he said after a moment. One of the women giggled again.

'Reckon it's time you was moving on,' said Tom Craddock, in a very unfriendly voice.

'When we're ready,' said the other man, offensive now. 'Much right here as you have.'

And then Tom Craddock moved across and sat down very heavily on one wing of the shiny new car. He was a big man—thirteen or fourteen stone perhaps. The car sagged: there was a dull twang as the metal began to buckle.

'Here,' said the man, 'you leave my car alone.' He stepped forward, angry. Tom Craddock sat, and took the pipe out of his pocket. The man, very red in the face, began to shout about calling the police. And then, out of the clear evening sky, a stone thumped on the roof of the car, leaving a little silver scar. There was no one to be seen except two very small girls at the far side of the pond and an old man on the bench under the oak tree. Tom Craddock began to re-light his pipe.

'Come on, George,' said one of the women, in a shrill, tight voice, 'I want to go.'

Tom Craddock got up, and watched them get into the car, the man still talking threateningly about the police, and then, as they drove away with a squeal of tyres, he went into the pub.

Peter and Mair, walking past the pond to go home,

thought they heard a soft rumble above their heads, as though someone closed a window.

Seven

'THEY'VE USED everything you can imagine!' said Peter excitedly. 'An old car, bedsteads, chicken coops, tree-trunks and I don't know what. Honestly, it's about five feet high, and they've put barbed wire all across the top. They must have been at it all night. You never saw anything like it!'

'Right across the lane?' said Mair, incredulous. 'So you can't get into the old village at all?'

'That's it. A huge great barricade. I don't think you could knock it down even with a bulldozer.'

Mr Jenkins, understandably perhaps, had disbelieved Peter's tale of a barricade erected in the night, and had got up from the breakfast table, tea undrunk and cornflakes uneaten, to investigate for himself. He came back ten minutes later.

'You're right, boy. By God, you're right. Now, there's an extraordinary thing! Cut themselves right off, they have, as though they don't want anyone coming in or out—unless they say so. There's just the pathway through the church-yard left—and the gate's shut at the far end with a chap standing by it, on the watch, as though they'll not let any-one through they don't want. Extraordinary, it is.'

They don't want any more strangers coming in and look-ing at them, thought Mair, laughing at them . . . They're just going to sit it out by themselves.

Yesterday's hazy sunshine had vanished. Instead, it was a day of high, gusty winds and running clouds. Under the chestnuts by the church the first conkers were scattered:

95

shiny brown glinting through white pith, and around the spire the rooks swirled, pushed and sucked by the wind like great black leaves. In a cottage garden a sheet flapped in the wind, making sharp cracks, and the corrugated-iron roof of a chicken-shed rattled and grumbled like distant thunder.

The barricade was all that Peter had said. At first, and if you had not known that the lane by the church led down to the green, you might have thought that you had taken a wrong turn and were facing some junk yard. An old car, without wheels or windows, gutted like the carcase of an animal, was planted in the centre as a base, and all

above and around it were heaped the discarded objects of Charlton Underwood's daily life: bedsteads trailing broken springs, mattresses speckled with green mildew, buckets without bottoms, a rusty iron boiler, dustbin lids, kettles, planks.

There was a considerable traffic along the path through the churchyard. At the far side, certainly, the cloth-capped head of whoever was minding the gate could just be seen above the wall, but people came and went and he took no notice—children, boys wheeling bikes, the postman, Mrs Leacock's sister from Long Barton, the carpenter repairing some broken slates on the pub roof. Peter and Mair went into the churchyard and looked over the wall. The level was several feet above that of the lane and the green, so that they could look down on the green, the pond and the houses. The wind had whipped the surface of the pond into corrugations, and the ducks were sheltering together in a huddle at one end. A small branch had broken off the oak tree and fallen onto the bench below. Somewhere a window had been left unfastened and was banging, but otherwise everything was very quiet. Indeed, there was hardly anyone about, except someone doing something to a bicycle wheel at the far side, and Evadne, knocking at a cottage door.

It was almost, Mair thought, as though everyone were dead. And then she wished she hadn't thought it.

On the other side of the barricade a small crowd had begun to gather, mostly people from the new estate, staring at the barricade and offering explanations and remarks.

'It's an epidemic,' said a woman with a pram, loudly. 'They've got an epidemic in there. That's what it is. An illness nobody ever heard of before.'

'If it was,' said someone else, 'the authorities would've done something, wouldn't they? The Health, and the Council, and them. They wouldn't just leave them to it, would they?'

'It's to keep us out,' said another woman. 'They always did resent the new estate. Funny lot, they are.'

'It's because of that bit in the paper,' Peter whispered to Mair, 'that was why the people in cars came.'

'I know. Beasts.'

'Anyway,' said a bald-headed man, 'whatever they've put it there for it won't be allowed to stay. Obstructing the highway—that's what they're doing. They've got no right.'

'Why?' said Mair, suddenly infuriated by his tone of righteous indignation. 'Do you want to go down there?'

'No,' said the man, turning to glare at her. 'But I might. Anyway, they've got no right.' He moved away, muttering something about no daughter of his going around in trousers, with her hair all anyhow.

Mair stuck her tongue out at his back. 'Interferer,' she said. 'Bossy. Bite him, Tar.' But Tar, who never did respond to situations, just wagged his tail ingratiatingly and went on watching a little boy eat an iced lolly.

And still there was neither sight nor sound from the other side of the barricade, except the top of that head just visible over the churchyard wall. The crowd began to dwindle, tired of waiting for something to happen. Peter and Mair decided to go through the churchyard and see if they too would be allowed to go onto the green like the village children. They were just about to do so when a disturbance behind made them look back. A lorry had turned into the lane and come to a halt in front of the barricade, brakes squealing. The crowd unfolded to give it room, and then closed round it, much interested.

The driver got down and studied the barricade.

'What's this then?' he said at last.

'You can't go no further,' said a woman.

'Who said? The Council didn't say nothing about the road being closed. I got a job to do down there. Inspection of drains and manhole covers.'

99

Now the children could see the neat lettering on the side of the lorry—Barton Rural District Council.

'They did it themselves,' offered another woman. 'There's something funny going on in there. They won't let no one in from outside.'

The lorry-driver stood staring in front of him in perplexity.

'Well,' said the bald man officiously, 'aren't you going to do something about it?'

'Don't know what I can do, mate,' said the driver. 'Can't go no further, can I, so it looks like I'll have to go back and tell 'em at the Council I couldn't get there.' He appeared to be happy with this solution and began to climb back into the lorry again. The crowd rustled, dissatisfied.

'You've been obstructed,' said the bald man. 'You'll have to report it to the police. Got to report an obstruction to the police, it's the law.'

The driver looked down at him doubtfully, engine throbbing. 'I dunno,' he said.

'Well, I do,' said the bald man. 'And if you won't do anything I shall have to do it myself. I consider it my duty. I shall inform the police.' He turned and marched away. The crowd watched him go with interest.

Five minutes later he was back again. 'They're on their way,' he said importantly. 'Squad car from Barton.'

The lorry driver sighed. 'I could of done it another day, mate,' he said wearily. 'No need for all this.'

'They've got no right,' said the bald man firmly, stationing himself in a strategic position by the barricade. They all waited silently in the sunshine. Overhead the rooks cawed, and somewhere on the estate a milk-float purred on its rounds.

At last the police-car arrived and two policemen got out and walked over to the barricade. The bald man watched in triumph. 'Soon bring them to their senses now,' he said.

The policemen inspected the barricade, and consulted

with each other in low voices. The women with prams, and the bald man, all swayed forward slightly in an attempt to overhear. Then one of the policemen turned and went quickly through the churchyard, past Peter and Mair. He opened the gate and they heard him speak to the man on the other side. 'Morning, Bill. What's going on here, then?' The rest of the conversation was inaudible. After a few minutes the policeman came back. This time he spoke loudly enough for everyone to hear.

'Seems they don't want no traffic down to the green. Seems there's been a lot of cars and they don't like it. They say the road don't go anywhere except the green so there's no need for anyone to go down it.'

'They can't do that,' said the other policeman. 'There's essential services and that. And it's a public thoroughfare.'

'They say they'll let anything essential through. Fire-engines and the post—that kind of thing.'

'It's not true,' said an anonymous voice from the crowd. 'They've got an epidemic, that's what. Only they aren't letting on.'

'What's that?' said the policeman sharply.

'Doctor was down there yesterday,' said another voice.

'That's right,' said the bald man. 'In and out of a lot of houses, he was.' He stared accusingly at the policemen.

'Well, that's all right then, isn't it?' said one of them. 'There can't be any epidemic. If there was anything funny like that going on we'd have been told, and we haven't heard anything official, so that's all right then.'

The crowd looked disappointed.

'All the same,' said the other policeman briskly, 'it can't stay there, even if it's doing no harm. That's the law. We'll report back to headquarters and they'll arrange for it to be taken down, if they won't do it themselves.' They moved back towards the car.

'Will there be prosecutions?' said the bald man hopefully.

'I wouldn't know, sir,' said the policeman in a leve voice.

When they had gone the crowd began to disperse, since it was apparent that nothing more was to happen for the moment. Peter and Mair came out of the churchyard and set off slowly down the road towards the estate. They met Evadne, on foot, coming up a narrow lane that led round the back of the church to the green.

'The police are going to have it pulled down,' said Mair dejectedly, 'all because of a beastly nosy man. I think it's mean—why shouldn't they shut the road if they want to? Why should they have to put up with people coming in and laughing at them?'

'Too right,' said Evadne, 'but they might have seen it coming, if they'd only thought. Still, I wouldn't be too surprised if they haven't got something else up their sleeves. Be interesting to see. They're in a funny state: half of them's really frightened of what they think's happening and the other half's forgotten what all the fuss is about and are just enjoying having a go at Them.'

'Them?' said Mair.

'Everyone who isn't Us. Everyone outside the village. Honestly—it's like a siege in there, and everyone friends with everyone else. People who haven't spoken for ten years giving each other cups of tea, and old Tom Craddock buying drinks at the pub for all and sundry, who wouldn't give you a smile on a wet Sunday in the normal way of things.'

'Any news of Goacher?' said Peter.

Evadne shook her head. 'I was down at the farm early. They've still not seen him. Betsy's about the same. Poorly. And I had the feeling she's got something on her mind, poor kid, but she won't tell anyone what it is.'

'Somebody ought to find Goacher,' said Mair, 'and then he could put the chalice back and everything would be all right. Why doesn't anybody?'

But Peter and Evadne had turned away, talking about something else.

After lunch things began to happen. A lorry appeared, heralded by a goggled and gloved policeman on a motor-bike, and drew up in front of the barricade. Five workmen got out and proceeded, slowly and with much difficulty, to dismantle the barricade and pile it into the back of the lorry, superintended by the policeman and watched by two interested groups of spectators, one from the housing estate and one from within the old village. The group from the housing estate was complacent, with a general air of I-told-you-so. Inside, the old villagers* watched quietly, expressionless. They made no attempt either to impede or to help. The barricade gave the workmen a good deal of trouble: iron bedsteads, wire-netting and the old car had become firmly entangled with one another and had to be cut apart with blow-torches.

'Should have brought a bull-dozer,' said the bald-headed man with satisfaction.

At last the job was done and the lorry departed. The lane down to the green was clear once again. The bald man walked up and down it several times, as though to prove something. Then he went home.

In the later afternoon several of the mothers from the housing estate walked down to the old village and pushed their prams round the pond, but withdrew indignantly after a plump baby had been hit on the head by a falling conker. There was a lot of discussion about whether it had dropped or been thrown: certainly it was still very windy.

And then, at about six o'clock, a dark green van and a small red car swept up the main road and turned smartly down the lane to the green. Within minutes the word had got around the estate.

'It's the telly. There's a man from the telly down in the old village.'

When Peter and Mair got down there the van had

disgorged two men in shirtsleeves and a lot of trailing cables, which they were busy draping around the pond and the bench under the oak tree, watched by a growing crowd. A third man, in suede jacket and dark glasses, was walking up and down, looking at the houses and elbowing people out of his way.

'I want a shot of these crosses,' the children heard him say. 'And tell that old dear to take her washing down: it's distracting.' The shirt-sleeved men ran back and forth, littering the green with cables, and tall cameras on wheels. They peered at the suede-jacketed man from behind the cameras, and the suede-jacketed man dabbed at his hair with a comb and then walked backwards in a practised way, smiling and talking at the cameras. Several men came out of the pub to watch. They stood staring, beer-mugs in their hands.

'I'll talk us in,' said the suede-jacketed man, 'and then we'll have one or two spot interviews.' He threw a quick glance at the crowd. His eye fell on Mair. 'Would you like to go and stand by that door, dear? The one with the cross on it. Make a nice shot, wouldn't it, Leslie?—The girl with the hair and that frightfully olde-worlde cottage.'

'No,' said Mair coldly, 'I won't.'

Suede jacket looked surprised. 'All right, dear, suit yourself. Ready, Leslie? Let's go, then.' He stood in front of the camera and began to talk to it in a pleasant, conversational voice.

'Here in this sleepy Cotswold village of Charlton Underwood things are not quite as calm as they seem. I'm standing on the old village green, with the pond behind me'—the camera swung away for a moment to close in on two ducks and an empty jam-jar bobbing up and down on the water—'and in front of me the four hundred-year-old village pub. Charlton Underwood is a pleasant backwater, scarcely touched by the twentieth century, and many of the village families have lived here for generations. Everything is quiet here now, but this morning there were strange scenes in the little lane which joins the old village to the main road. It seems that the villagers had erected a barricade during the night to keep all traffic from coming down here, and were refusing to let strangers into the village. The barricade was removed on the instructions of the Chief Constable, who refused to make any comment when we spoke to him this afternoon. "Around and About in the Midlands" is anxious to hear from the villagers themselves why they want to cut themselves off, and what, if anything, has happened here. Let us hear what the people of Charlton Underwood have to say.'

Trailing microphone and cable, he moved over to the group outside the pub, and held it out to an elderly man. 'I wonder if you'd care to let us have your thoughts, sir?'

The man mumbled something.

'I beg your pardon?' said suede jacket.

' 'E says 'e don't do no thinkin',' said one of the other men, loudly.

'Oh.' Suede jacket snatched the microphone away hurriedly and held it out to Tom Craddock. 'What about you, sir? Have your family lived here a long time?'

Tom Craddock took a long swill at his beer, and wiped his mouth with the back of his hand. 'They might have,' he said slowly, 'and then again they might not have.'

A flicker of irritation crossed the interviewer's expressionless face. 'I wonder if you could tell us why this barricade was put up?'

Tom Craddock looked thoughtful. Finally he said, 'I could. But I don't reckon as I'm going to.'

'Cut, Leslie!' snapped suede jacket. He glared at Tom Craddock and moved away, almost tripping over a cable that snaked across the road. 'We'll try the women. They always love the idea of seeing themselves on the box.' He walked over to the group by the cottage, pursued by the cameraman.

'Could you tell us about this barricade?' he said, approaching a stout woman standing beside Evadne.

The woman stared unresponsively for a moment, then she turned to Evadne and said in a clearly audible whisper: 'What's 'e got them funny glasses on for?' Evadne giggled.

'Oh, *cut* for heaven's sake!' said suede jacket in exasperation. 'All right, we'll have to do without the interviews. Thick-headed lot they are down here. Let's have me in front of the pond now, with the church behind.' He backed away, conversing with the camera once more.

'It's a little difficult to read the minds of the villagers, as Charlton Underwood sleeps on in the September sunshine, the spire of the fourteenth century church rising behind the delightful cluster of age-old cottages, but one thing is for certain, there is something strange going on in this typically English village. I wonder if . . .'

But they were not to hear what it was he wondered. A group of the men outside the pub had drawn close to the cameraman as he advanced on the suede-jacketed man, as though fascinated by what was going on. And all of a sudden a foot shot out, making the cameraman stumble and fall with a muffled cry. The wheeled camera continued on its own, and the suede-jacketed man, oblivious of what had happened, continued to retreat, talking as he went. The crowd watched with interest. The cameraman scrambled to his feet and shouted 'Watch it, Julian!' But too late. The suede-jacketed man had taken a final step backwards into the pond: there was a loud splash, and a second as the camera toppled in after him.

Nobody laughed. The woman beside Evadne said disapprovingly: 'It's mucky, that old pond. 'E were silly to get in there.' The men went back into the pub, holding empty beer-mugs, and the rest of the crowd filtered slowly away, back into houses or up the lane past the church.

The camera and the suede-jacketed man, both dripping mud and green slime, were extracted from the pond. Five minutes later the two cars drove away.

'Serve them right,' said Evadne with satisfaction. 'That'll teach them to come sticking their noses in other people's business. Pity that reporter from the paper didn't go the same way, then maybe we'd have had none of this bother.'

'What'll they do now?' said Peter.

'I don't know, love. Nothing, I hope. If people will only leave us alone. Off you go now, I've got a couple of calls to make before I have my tea.'

The children sat awhile on the bench under the oak tree, watching the sun go down behind the church, and the stone of the houses turn to blazing gold in the evening light. Nothing happened, and nobody took any notice of them. Presently they got up and walked away up the lane towards the road. But just as they turned the corner a car, approaching hesitantly, swung round the corner and down to the green. Faces stared at them out of the window.

It didn't look as though Charlton Underwood was going to be left alone for long.

They must have been hard at it most of the night, digging the trench. It was a neat section out of the lane down to the green, wall to wall, a good four feet across and perhaps two feet deep. Of course there was no tarmac on the lane, otherwise, as Peter pointed out, they couldn't have done it without a pneumatic drill. Even so, the core of stones and rubble must have created quite a problem: they were piled up now in a big heap on the far side. Against it leaned a plank, which came into use every time someone wanted to leave the village.

'Like a drawbridge,' said Mair admiringly. 'They think of everything.'

Water had seeped up into the bottom of the trench. Now it was almost half full, brown, with a rainbow sheen of oil on top. You wouldn't fancy walking through it, except perhaps in boots.

'All the same,' said Peter despondently, 'the police'll soon deal with that, won't they? They've only got to bulldoze the stuff back in. You wait and see.'

He was right. By eleven o'clock that morning the squad car had been and gone, and a bright yellow council bulldozer had come clanking and grinding up the main road from Barton driven by an expressionless man to whom, presumably, it was a job like any other. For an hour or so the bulldozer crawled back and forth like some ungainly prehistoric animal and by twelve the only indication of where the trench had been was a wide band of muddy surface across the lane. A number of people from the new estate came to watch, but the old village was strangely silent. A few of the children could be seen, but otherwise there seemed to be no one about at all, except one or two old men sunning themselves on the seat by the pond, and Evadne on her morning round.

And after lunch the sightseers were back. A trickle of cars, drifting aimlessly down the lane to the green, round the pond, pausing for a moment, and then driving away again to the main road. Sometimes people got out and wandered around, pointing and staring. They dropped cigarette packets around the green and threw sweet papers and iced lolly sticks into the pond. And Charlton Underwood ignored them. It might have been an empty village. Nobody came or went from the cottages round the green: the shop and the pub had bolted and barred their doors. Everything was silent. The sightseers grew bolder. They even crept up cottage paths and peered in at the windows. A woman picked herself a bunch of flowers from one of the front gardens.

'How can they!' exploded Mair. 'How would they like it if it was their village!'

The children spent most of the afternoon sitting under

the churchyard wall, watching and simmering. But there was nothing they could do about it. Once a man got out of a car and came over to speak to them.

'Live here, do you?' he said, shifting a cigarette from one corner of his mouth to the other.

Peter nodded sullenly while Mair looked straight in front of her, aloof.

'Nice place, is it?' he persisted.

'It was till you came here,' muttered Mair. Then she said aloud, rudely, 'Did you want something?'

'Just having a bit of a look round,' he said casually. 'Read in the paper they'd been having a bit of trouble here. Thought we'd come along and see the fun, but it's as dead as a doornail.'

Mair was about to say more when a woman leaned out of a car and shouted 'Come on, Ted, no point in hanging around here. There's nothing to see.' The man moved off. Mair pushed the hair out of her eyes and glowered at him until he got into the car and drove away.

'Where *is* everybody, then?' Peter said once, and Mair shrugged.

'Inside the houses, I suppose.'

At about five o'clock they decided to go home. It had been a thoroughly depressing afternoon.

'If I was them,' said Mair venomously, 'the villagers, I mean, I'd spread tacks all over the road and puncture their tyres.'

'Then they'd be there all the longer,' Peter pointed out.

Just past the church, on the same side as the old village but a little beyond it, there was a very small Methodist chapel, set back from the road in its own neglected, overgrown grounds. It was a neat building, like a model house, with two pointed windows at each side, white double doors facing the road, and a little white plaque on one side that said 'Wesley's Chapel 1805'. Mair had always liked it: for one thing it reminded her of the chapels at home in Wales, though the stone was a different colour and the windows were a prettier shape. As they passed it now, they were surprised to see people filing in through the open doors, mostly men, but with a sprinkling of women.

'Funny time for a service,' said Peter. 'Middle of Friday afternoon.'

The road bent round towards their own estate, so that the wall that enclosed the chapel's yard came into view, feet deep in long grass and draped with ivy. Peter, looking back, said in surprise: 'Look, there's Evadne!'

'What on *earth* is she doing?' said Mair.

For Evadne appeared to be trying to climb over the wall. She was wearing a cotton dress instead of her uniform, and sandals, and was trying desperately to get a toe-hold on the loose stones of the six foot wall. She scrabbled and slithered in an ungainly way, throwing anxious glances over her shoulder from time to time, and at last, using a strand of ivy as a rope, managed to pull herself up, straddle the top, and vanish over the other side into the chapel yard.

'I say!' said Mair excitedly, 'I bet she's found Goacher! That's what it is—he must be hiding there with the chalice and she's found out somehow. Clever Evadne! Let's go and see.'

They left the road and crossed a piece of waste land to the wall. They climbed over it, finding it rather easier than Evadne had ('I expect she doesn't climb walls much nowadays,' said Mair kindly) and dropped down into the yard, where the grass was waist-high. There were still one or two people coming up the path to the chapel; and the children ducked down to keep out of sight, deciding that if Evadne had chosen this unorthodox way in she must have some good reason for wanting no one to see her, and they'd better do the same. They waited until there seemed to be no one else to come, and then made their way along the side of the wall towards the back of the chapel. There had been no sign of Evadne so far, but as soon as the back of

110

the chapel came into view they saw her. She was standing up, still nearly waist-high in the grass that reached right up to the sides of the building, and trying vainly to get a hold with her finger-tips on the sloping outer sill of a high, slit window in the wall.

'I can't see Goacher anywhere,' said Peter, puzzled.

'She seems to be trying to climb up that wall now,' said Mair. 'We'd better go and help.'

They stood up and waded through the grass towards Evadne. As soon as she heard them she let go of the sill and swung round nervously, guilt written all over her face; but when she saw who it was her expression changed to one of extreme irritation. She began waving wildly at them.

'I think she's saying "Go away",' said Peter, stopping.

'No, she isn't. She's saying "Come and help me".'

As soon as they were within earshot Evadne hissed furiously, 'You little fools! You'll give me away. What do you want?'

'We thought you'd found Goacher. Sorry, Evadne.'

'Well, now you're here you'll have to stay. Get down in the grass by the chapel.'

They all three crouched down against the wall. 'What are you doing, Evadne?' said Mair humbly.

'Something I never did in my life before,' Evadne was very terse, 'eavesdropping. And I don't like doing it, I can tell you. But I've got to.'

'Why?'

'Because they're up to something in the village. The men, mostly. And nobody'll tell me anything. They're treating me as if I was a stranger. Just because I brought the doctor in, and I was only doing my job.' She sounded hurt and offended.

'What's it all about?' said Peter eagerly.

'Something they've been planning since the police dealt with their barricade and the trench. They were meeting in the pub this morning, and now again here. They won't stand for much more, but I'm worried. I'm afraid they're going to go too far. That's why I'm here. If I knew what it was they were planning maybe I could still get them to be sensible. Can you help me get up on that sill?'

The sill was sloping, narrowing upwards towards the slit window, not more than nine inches or so at the narrowest point. Peter looked at Evadne's plump figure doubtfully.

'Mair's thinner,' he said at last. 'I think you might fall off.'

Evadne gave him a look. 'Thanks very much,' she said. 'All right, then. We'll have to give her a leg up.'

Between them they managed to heave Mair up high enough to get a grip on the edge of the sill, six feet or so above the ground, and then drag herself further up it, kicking wildly with her legs, until she was crouched uncomfortably, tending to slide backwards all the time.

'You'll have to be ready to catch me,' she whispered down to them. 'There's practically nothing to hold on to and if I slip I'll fall.'

'All right,' said Evadne impatiently, 'we're here. But tell us what you can see, and if you can hear what they say.'

Mair edged right up to the window until she could press one eye against the slit. For a moment she thought that the dark shape of her would be obvious from inside, and then remembered that the window was against a background of trees, so that she was presumably just part of a general shadow. She was looking straight down the centre of the chapel, though she could not see either side of it because of the narrowness of the slit. There was a stone floor and rush-seated chairs which had been unceremoniously stacked away at one end, and thirty or forty people standing around in groups, talking in low voices. It reminded her again of the chapels back in Wales. But it was clearly not a service that was going on. At the far end, beside the stacks of chairs, there was a pile of what, on closer inspec-

112

tion, she realised were long sticks, poles, and even several very ancient rifles. As she watched, a man came into the chapel and added another to the collection. And beside them stood a very strange-looking object made of rusty iron with two rows of gigantic interlocking teeth, like enormous combs, mounted on a base attached to a long, heavy chain. Two men stood looking down at it and she heard one say to the other with relish: 'That'll make 'em jump, eh, Bill?'

Mair slid back down the wall, ripping the front of her shirt and grazing her hands in the process. She reported what she'd seen in an excited whisper.

'What's the thing with teeth?' she finished. 'And what's it all about?'

Evadne was looking more and more distressed. 'Silly, pig-headed lot,' she spluttered. 'What good do they think it'll do them! That's a man-trap, my love, the old man-trap that's been in the pub cellar ever since I can remember, that used to be used to catch poachers in the old days. Nasty thing. And the rest's what they look like, sticks and guns.'

'They're going to keep people out themselves,' said Peter, in an awed voice. 'Is that it?'

'Good for them!' said Mair.

'Don't be silly,' snapped Evadne. 'Nobody's going to stand for private armies in this day and age, right or wrong. Just let them fire one of those rifles and they're going to pile up a whole load of trouble for themselves. It's one thing pushing men from the telly into the pond but it's quite another letting off rifles at people.'

'He wasn't pushed: he fell,' said Mair.

'Well, whichever it was. Anyway, it won't do. It's got to be stopped. Get up there again, there's a good girl, and see if you can hear anything.'

Mair scrambled up on to the sill once more and pressed her head up against the slit. The big doors had been closed now, and the pile of sticks and rifles had grown still more.

There was even a mysterious cannon-like object that might well have seen service at the battle of Waterloo. And things were going on now. A large, burly man, whom Mair recognised as Tom Craddock even though he had his back to her, was speaking.

'. . . We got a tidy few weapons, one way and another. Good thing some of us hung on to our Home Guard outfits. Now the way I look at it is this: we puts a line of stick men at the bottom of the lane, by the church, and then we has our riflemen behind them, across the green, and they doesn't shoot unless they has to.'

'What do we shoot at, Tom?' said a voice.

'You shoots where you like,' said Tom heavily. 'But we ain't aimin' at no bloodshed. We just wants to scare 'em off. Anyways, the kind of shot you are, Bill Turner, you wouldn't be likely to hit nothing.' Several people laughed.

A woman said timidly 'Police is going to come, isn't they, Tom? What do we do then?'

Several voices began to shout angrily.

'The police is with Them, anyways, they never did nothing for us, did they?'

'Police don't have no guns, do they?'

'They won't dare do nothing to us: we got a right to protect our property, haven't we?'

A man got up on a chair and shouted: 'The police should 'a stopped 'em coming down to make a nuisance of themselves in our village, and then we wouldn't 'a had to protect ourselves.' And there was a murmur of approval all round.

Tom Craddock rapped his stick on the floor for silence. 'We don't want nobody doing nothing foolish,' he bellowed. 'Police aren't allowed to lay hands on you so long as you don't hurt nobody. Leastways I don't reckon as they can,' he went on confusedly, 'but we don't want no fightin'. We just wants to keep us to ourselves and no more o' them strangers muckin' up our village.'

114

'No harm in letting off at a few rooks,' said one of the younger men pleadingly, caressing one of the rusty rifles.

'We'll see about that when the time comes.'

There was some more talk, and arrangements made for the distribution of the weapons, and then the meeting began to break up. Mair slithered down the wall again to report to the others.

'Gosh!' said Peter, wide-eyed. 'They really are going it, aren't they?'

'Funny thing is,' Mair added, 'that nobody once mentioned the chalice, or the Black Death, or any of that. It was as though they'd forgotten what it had all been about in the first place.'

'They have, most of them,' said Evadne. 'It's turned into something quite different. A chance to have a bash at things they don't like, such as the police, and strangers, and people telling them they've got to do this, that or the other. Charlton people have always been independent types. Oh, it's not that they weren't fussed about the illness in the first place, some of them, but one thing's led to another. But this won't do at all: just let a few of the young chaps get carried away and start waving those rifles around and the next thing we know we're going to have somebody getting hurt and half the village getting themselves clapped in prison. Silly lot they are.' She looked thoroughly distressed.

'What are we to do?' said Mair. They were all three still crouched down in the long grass. Mair's legs and arms were all pink-speckled where she had grazed them on the stone.

'I could talk to them—to old Tom and the others,' said Evadne doubtfully. 'Let on I know what they're up to. But I don't reckon they'd listen. After all I'm a girl, and they've known me since I was so high. No, there's no point. Only thing really is to get old Goacher back with that wretched cup, and bring the Tranters to their senses, and then they'll all snap out of it and things'll go back to normal and we won't get all these outsiders trailing around.'

The chapel had emptied now and the last of the villagers had disappeared down the road. Evadne and the children emerged cautiously from the yard. At the gate they separated, Evadne going in the direction of the old village and the children towards the estate.

They passed the track leading to the farm. The rain had almost washed the chalk cross off the wooden sign, but it was still faintly there, if you knew what to look for. In the distance the wood lay crouched and still, except for the ripples of changing light that ran across it as the wind stirred the leaves. Mair listened intently, but the bells were silent tonight.

'Look!' said Peter suddenly. High above the wood and the field something was drifting against the sky, sometimes still, backing against the wind, and then making great, deliberate, sweeping circles. It was the hawk.

'It's looking for food,' said Peter. 'I hope it finds something.' The great bird soared, and then swept down low towards them, so near that they could see the feathers at the tips of its wings spread out like dark fingers. Then it lifted again, flapped once or twice, and slid effortlessly away beyond the wood and out of sight.

'You know what,' said Peter, 'it's time someone looked for Goacher and brought the chalice back. No one else seems to be going to, so it'll have to be us. Tomorrow. All right?'

Mair nodded. That's what we should have done in the first place, she thought, instead of just watching things happen.

Eight

'YOU LOOK as though you're going on a safari,' said Mair, with some scorn.

It was true. Peter had with him two penknives and a torch, making the pockets of his anorak sag at either side: there was also a ball of string, a compass, a bag of boiled sweets, and the map, which he had to carry since it would not go in his pocket. Mair had nothing, except a sweater tied round her waist by the sleeves to save the bother of carrying it.

Peter had pored over the map most of last evening, face down on the kitchen floor.

'What do you want a map for?' said Mair in amazement. 'I mean, he won't be far, will he? Not Goacher—Betsy said he never goes far. Not far enough to need a map, you idiot.'

'It's not a distance map, stupid. If you knew anything about maps you'd see that. It's the two and a half inch Ordnance Survey.'

'Well, I still don't see how a map's going to help us find him.'

'Because,' said Peter patiently, 'I can find out from the map first the sort of places he might have gone to—the sort of places where he could hide. Quarries, disused railway cuttings, woods—that kind of thing.'

Mair looked over his shoulder. The tracery of lines and curves was utterly confusing at first. 'Oh,' she said, as the light dawned, 'the little squares are fields, and the dotted lines are paths. And the bits with dear little trees are woods. And the squiggly blue line's a stream.'

'*Aren't* you bright . . . These dear little trees here, as you call them, are Astercote wood, and here's the path down to the farm, and there's the farm, and all this side round the farm is fields and open country, so I don't reckon we should look there. It's the other side I'm interested in. Here, where it says "Quarry (disused)"—that might be a place to look, and this copse here, and this one over here. That's about a mile and a half from here—a bit more perhaps.'

So now they were on their way to start the search. They went first to the wood, partly to make sure that there was still no sign of Goacher there, and partly because Peter had spotted a footpath on the map which emerged from the far side of the wood and would take them conveniently to the quarry and copses he had decided to search. They plunged noisily through the wood, making no attempt at conceal-ment, calling as they went, and visiting both the clearing where Goacher usually spent his time, and the oak tree where the chalice had been. He was not there, though The Bitch came out to meet them. When Mair went to pat her she backed away growling, and they had to leave her, regretfully.

'I wonder why she stays,' said Peter.

'She thinks she's guarding it. Probably Goacher told her to.'

They found the right footpath, Peter making elaborate and rather unnecessary use of the compass. But when the trees finally thinned out and they found themselves at the edge of the wood, they were confronted not by a convenient dotted line but a pathless field of corn ending, distantly, in a blank hedge.

'Very useful map,' said Mair, with a touch of malice. 'Now what?'

Peter spread the map out on the ground and began to study it worriedly. 'Maybe we took the wrong path through the wood. No—because these fields are going upwards, and

118

that's what they should be doing to fit in with the contour lines, and that's east all right . . . It must just be that the path's been ploughed up. We'll have to try to get along by the hedge.'

They climbed a gentle hill, following the line of the hedge across two fields. They found a gap to scramble through out of the first field, and the second was easier since the corn had been cut and they could walk easily across among the scattered blocks of straw. Once at the top of the hill, Peter was able to feel confident once more.

'Look, I was right. There's the road, running along that way like it should be—and that must be Lower Barton village right over there. And there's this stream—where that line of willows is over there. And there's the copse we're aiming for.'

'And there's the path,' said Mair.

They were looking down into a shallow valley. A road wound like a flat grey ribbon down the centre of it, hidden here and there as the contours of the land changed, but always revealed by the movement of cars in each direction. On either side, golden fields of corn, some stubble, some not yet harvested, were criss-crossed by the dark green of hedges. Here and there the grey stone of a farmhouse or cottage could be seen among trees, or just topping a hedge, and the fist-shapes of a line of willows threaded across a water-meadow, following the banks of a hidden stream. On the horizon at one end of the valley a sudden activity of buildings, chimneys and telegraph wires indicated the out-skirts of Long Barton and at the other end was the dark smudge of the copse they were looking for. The path wound across a grass field, was hidden for a time by the willows and the stream, re-emerged, to be broken again by the road, and then merged into a line of hedges.

'What are we going to do when we find him?' said Mair, as they followed the trace of the path across the next field.

'Tell him what a commotion it's caused—him taking the

119

chalice away. If we can make him understand. And ask him to put it back where it was and then we can tell the Tranters, or ask Evadne to, and it'll soon get around to the village and then everything'll be all right again.'

'What if he won't?'

'I'm sure he will. After all he kept going on about it himself—how it must never be taken away from the wood. Funny, really, him doing it.'

The valley, once they were in it, seemed much wider than it had done from the top of the hill. It took them nearly half an hour to get to the copse, and when they finally got there it, too, was larger than they had expected, and presented an almost impenetrable tangle of bushes and undergrowth. They found one path leading right through it, and walked down this, calling 'Goacher, Goacher' and urging Tar to hunt among the brambles where they could not go.

'For once,' said Peter, 'that dog might actually be useful.'

But the copse was empty and silent. After quarter of an hour or so they decided to go on.

'There's this quarry,' said Peter, looking at the map again. 'It's not far. We could try there next.'

When they reached it Mair was disappointed. 'I thought quarries were all stones and cliffs,' she said. This one was a wide, shallow bowl, grass-covered and choked with high bramble thickets and small trees. Paths wound among the brambles, so that it was a kind of natural maze. Certainly an ideal place to hide.

'It's been out of use for years,' said Peter, 'so it's all over-grown. Come on, Mair, I've got a feeling this is going to be the place. Tar, go seek!'

Tar dashed off enthusiastically down the grassy slope into the brambles, followed by the children.

'Goacher!' called Peter. 'Goacher—are you there? It's only us. Don't be frightened. We've got something important to tell you.'

Silence, except for a blackbird which rushed off shrieking as Tar bounded out of a bush.

They threaded their way in and out of the brambles, separating, and meeting up with each other again unexpectedly. All of a sudden there came a hysterical barking from Tar.

'He's found something,' said Peter excitedly, and plunged off down another path, with Mair at his heels.

But it was just a dead sheep, a mound of dirty grey wool half under a bramble bush. Mair screamed and fled.

'It stank,' said Peter, when he caught up with her. 'That's all. Nothing to get in a state about.'

But Mair was still shuddering. 'I can't stand dead things.'

'Well, he's not here either. Tar would have found him.' Peter was beginning to sound a bit disconsolate. He unfolded the map again and spread it out on the grass. They both stared down at it.

'Where are we?' said Mair.

Peter pointed. 'Just there. And it's all fields for a long way now. There is a spinney over there: I suppose we could try that.'

'Millfield Ho,' said Mair, craning her neck sideways to read the small letters. 'That's just over there somewhere. Over the top of this hill, I suppose. What's a Ho?'

'Not a Ho, silly. House, it means. Millfield House. It must mean some big house. He wouldn't be anywhere near a house.'

'No, I suppose not.'

They climbed out of the quarry. At the top was a hedge, and on the other side of the hedge a big field, dotted with black and white cows, stretched away to a stand of chestnut trees in the distance. Through gaps in the trees they could see the frontage of a very big house. There were stone-mullioned windows and chimney stacks twisted like barley sugar. Mair stared with interest.

'No good going up there,' said Peter, turning away. 'Better try the opposite direction.'

'Wait,' said Mair suddenly. 'It isn't a proper house. It's just a front. It's ruined.'

Peter screwed his eyes irritably, and then gave up. 'All right, if you say so. I can't see that far. Anyway, what difference does it make?'

'Lots,' said Mair in excitement. 'It's just the kind of place . . . Come on.' She began to run across the field, and Peter, suddenly seeing what she meant, followed.

Fifty yards away they stopped, and stood looking at the house. It was a very strange place: there was this beautiful, elaborate front, with its great door, surmounted by stone carved roses and leaves, and each side a balanced arrangement of bow windows, complementing each other, with more stonework, and above, two more storeys of windows, and finally the stone coping and the twisted chimneys. But the whole thing was a shell: the roof had fallen in so that the rooms inside were open to the sky, and through the big, glassless windows they could see young trees growing, pushing through the stonework and tearing apart the bricks. The chestnut plantation spread right up to the walls of the house, and the wind sighed and moaned through the branches. Sheep grazed under the trees and as they watched one wandered through the gaping door into the house.

'Gosh!' said Peter, impressed.

They went up to the house, warily. The sheep grazed all round them, and rooks swirled above the chestnuts, but the wind blowing in at the empty windows and gusting up and down the great, tumbling walls made uncanny whistlings and sighings. It was not an entirely comfortable place: it might very well conceal the unexpected.

They peered in at one of the ground floor windows. Inside, the floors had all fallen in: the walls soared clear up to the sky with empty fireplaces stuck awkwardly here and there. There were mounds of rubble, and the stone was speckled with bird droppings. Pigeons roosted in gaps in the stonework. Plucking up courage, they climbed over the window-sill and advanced cautiously into what had been a room. A blank square that had once been a door led on into another room. They were almost through that, picking their way carefully over the rubble, when there was a violent disturbance from beyond as a big, heavy body moved suddenly.

With a yell, Mair was out of the window and fleeing into the chestnuts.

Two minutes later Peter came to fetch her, shaking with laughter. 'It was a cow. As surprised as you were. She's gone now.'

They returned to the house, Mair keeping several yards behind this time. The front door led straight into a big hall: it was strange to stand in the middle of it with the great stone fireplace still in the wall on one side, smoke-blackened, and overhead the sky and the trees and the rooks and the sighing wind.

The end wall had collapsed almost completely, showing the fields beyond. Mair walked across and looked out.

'There's been a garden once,' she said. 'You can see where there's been hedges and paving stones.' But brambles and saplings had engulfed it now, and the sheep roamed over what had perhaps been a lawn. Fifty yards away from the house stood an octagonal stone building with high, glassless windows. A flight of shallow steps led up to it. Mair pointed at it and said tensely, 'Peter—look at that!'

'It's some kind of summer-house. What about it?'

'There's someone in there. I saw a face at the window. It's gone now.'

They scrambled through a gap in the wall and crept along under an overgrown hedge towards the summer-house. Mair was holding Tar under one arm. 'Just in case it isn't what we think . . .'

At the bottom of the steps they paused. From somewhere inside the building came a very low growl.

'Fang,' murmured Peter. 'At least I hope so.' Then he said quietly, 'Goacher. Goacher—is that you in there?'

Something moved. Again the growl.

'Goacher. We won't hurt you. Do come out.'

There was a shuffling on the stone floor, and Goacher's round face appeared in the doorway, the blue eyes blinking in the sunlight. Fang slunk out behind him, still growling in his throat.

The children sighed with relief.

'Thank goodness,' said Peter. 'We were afraid it wasn't. I say, you do have a thing about ruins, don't you? But never mind. What did you go off for—you've no idea the bother there's been in the village.'

Goacher squatted down on the steps and began to whimper. 'I were afraid to tell 'un. I were scared—scared of what they'd say and scared of what was to happen. I knows what 'ud happen if it were to leave Astercote.'

'It's all right,' said Mair soothingly, 'they are all in a bit of a state about it, but all you've got to do is put it back and nobody'll say anything about it.'

Goacher squinted and shook. 'I can't put 'un back,' he moaned.

'Why not?' said Peter. 'Have you got it here? Look, if you're scared to, we'll put it back for you. Honest—nobody's going to do anything to you.'

Goacher stared at them stupidly. 'I can't put 'un back,' he repeated. 'I didn't take 'un. I found 'un gone and I were scared to tell so I come here to hide.'

The children looked at each other, aghast.

'If he didn't take it,' said Mair at last, 'then who did?'

Nine

THE POLICEMAN listened, his face expressionless. He only interrupted once.

'You say there was just you and your sister there when the lad from the farm showed you this cup?'

'That's it,' said Peter unhappily. The story sounded more and more improbable.

'And you say as far as you know no one else has ever seen it except Mr Tranter, and the little girl.'

Peter nodded.

'And all this business in the village is because of the cup being taken? Building barricades and digging up the road and all?'

'It's because of the Black Death,' Mair burst in. 'They think they've got it. At least some of them do. And they hate people coming in and staring at them.'

The policeman looked at her sternly. 'Now, young woman, that doesn't sound a very likely tale, does it? I heard different: seems they've always been a tricky lot in Charlton and they didn't like the new building here. But they got to learn to live with that, haven't they?'

Peter was very red in the face. It had been his idea that they should tell the police: Mair had said all along that they wouldn't believe him, and now it looked as though she was right, and he wished he'd never begun.

'You do know, don't you,' said the policeman, 'about the Tranter lad? Him that hangs around the wood. You know he's a bit—well, a bit weak-headed?'

'Yes,' said Mair passionately, 'of course we know. But it

did happen. Honestly it did. We wouldn't make up a story like that.' She glared at the policeman through a curtain of blowing hair. They had come straight from finding Goacher, all muddy and dishevelled: the policeman was standing by the church wall, arms folded, presumably to prevent anything else being built or dug.

'Hmmmn. Well, I'll tell you what I'll do. I'll tell them back at the station what you just told me and I daresay they'll send a man down to have a word with Mr Tranter. That do?'

Mair turned away, scowling. 'I know what Mr Tranter'll say,' she muttered.

'Thank you very much,' said Peter. All he wanted to do now was get away.

The policeman came round to the house that evening. Peter and Mair, lurking behind the kitchen door, heard him in the hall, talking to their father. The conversation had begun ominously with the policeman saying 'I wonder if I could have a word with you, sir. It's about your lad and his sister.' They hadn't been able to catch everything that followed except odd snatches. '. . . Bit fanciful, are they? Apt to imagine things and that?' And their father saying 'The girl is. Lives in a world of her own. But there's no harm in it.' And then they'd chatted on, quite friendly, and the children heard them laugh a bit, and finally the policeman said 'Well, thank you for clearing that up, sir. I thought it must be a bit of a joke when Mr Tranter at the farm said there wasn't anything in it.' And then the front door closed.

Their father came into the kitchen, stern-faced. 'Now, Mair, what's been going on? Have you been telling stories to the policeman? Lucky for you he was a nice, easy-going chap.'

'I didn't,' said Mair sulkily. 'It wasn't a story. It's true.'

'No harm in telling yourself stories, girl. But keep them to yourself. Don't go bothering policemen. It's cheeky.

Specially just now when they've got all this trouble down in the old village. You shouldn't let her put you up to things, Peter.'

Peter opened his mouth to speak, and then shut it again. What's the use? he thought.

Mr Jenkins was talking to their mother about the old village. 'Bit tactless, you know,' he was saying, 'sticking these new estates on to an old village like that. Bound to cause feeling. Seems they want to cut off the green completely—stop anyone going down there. That's going too far, I'd say.'

You've got it all wrong, thought Mair balefully. They don't care tuppence about the new estate. She signalled to Peter to come out into the garden.

They conferred in whispers outside the back door. 'If we don't do something, nobody else will,' said Mair. 'We've got to find who took it. The police don't believe it ever existed and Mr Tranter doesn't want to have anything to do with them so he says it doesn't too. So that only leaves us and Goacher who've seen it—and nobody's going to take any notice of anything Goacher says.'

'Or us either,' said Peter gloomily.

'Exactly. So we've got to do it on our own. And bring it back to Astercote.'

'It's all very well saying that. How?'

Mair stopped, crestfallen. 'I don't know.'

They stood for a few moments in silence. It was dusk. Lights began to come on in the houses round, and the blue flicker of television sets.

'Let's go and see Evadne,' said Peter. 'At least we can tell her we found Goacher.'

Mair put her head in at the sitting-room door. 'We're taking Tar for a walk,' she said frostily. There was no answer, except a grunt from her father.

There was a different policeman on duty outside the church. He gave them a sharp look as they passed. Mair sailed by, her nose in the air, thinking: I hope you've got to stand there all night and I hope it pours with rain.

The green seemed fairly quiet, except for a group of boys on motor-bikes hovering around the oak tree, and the sound of glasses clinking through the open window of the pub. There were no cars.

Evadne was drinking tea in her kitchen, shoes off, stockinged feet propped on a chair, her hair untidy and her face pink and shiny. The children burst in without knocking.

'We've found him!' said Mair.

'But he hasn't got it,' Peter went on. 'It wasn't him that took it. He ran away because he was scared when he found it had gone. We found him at that old ruined house.'

Evadne put down her cup, looking shocked. 'Well I never!' she said. 'It's been pinched, then. Now, who'd do a thing like that? Mind, I daresay it's worth a packet.'

'Someone who needs money,' said Mair.

'Who doesn't?' said Evadne, frowning.

'There aren't any sightseers this evening,' said Peter, looking out of the window. 'Maybe it's blowing over.'

'There wouldn't be,' said Evadne. 'There's a fair on at Barton. Alternative attraction. We won't get anyone around tonight, I'll be bound, but tomorrow it'll be the same. And it's tomorrow they're planning their little demonstration for—Tom Craddock and the others. Regular arms dump they've got stacked up in the pub.'

The children looked at each other in dismay. 'It'll be awful if they get themselves sent to prison,' said Mair, aghast. 'People like Mr Tranter and the others.'

'What time'll they do it?' said Peter.

'Oh, latish, I should think. When they're all back from work.'

Mair went over to the window and stood looking out at the green. Under the oak tree, the motor-bike boys were revving their engines, smoking, lounging about the road. She stared at them, and began to remember something.

'The point is,' Peter was saying earnestly, 'that if it's true Goacher never showed it to anyone else, then how did anyone else know where it was?'

Evadne snatched her feet off the chair, making the children jump. 'Goodness,' she exclaimed, 'I believe that's what Betsy must have been on about this morning, and yesterday, when I was down there. She's not much better, and I thought she was feverish. She kept saying over and over something about "It wasn't just them, it was Luke too," and "Luke kept asking and Goacher took him there to stop him bothering him." I didn't take any notice—I was busy thinking of other things.'

'Luke!' cried Mair. 'Of course!'

The motor-bike boys had put on helmets and goggles and were preparing to leave: the green throbbed with the roar of their engines. They looked like a fleet of spacemen, indistinguishable.

'He'll be with that mob,' said Evadne. 'Not that you can tell t'other from which.'

The motor-bikes roared round the green and up the lane, spraying gravel and blue exhaust.

'If he's got it,' said Peter urgently, 'he'll try to sell it, won't he? Perhaps he already has.' His face fell.

'I doubt it,' said Evadne. 'Look, it's not going to be an easy thing to sell, is it? He could try antique shops, but most of them would be suspicious, wouldn't they? They'd wonder how he came by a thing like that: most of them wouldn't want to buy stolen stuff. So he'd have to find someone not too fussy, wouldn't he? And that might take time. And he works at the garage all day—he'd only get Saturday off, and there hasn't been a Saturday since the thing went, has there?'

'So he may still have it?' said Mair excitedly.

'Listen,' said Evadne slowly. 'Luke has a room at Mrs Barnet's by the shop—that's where he lives. And I've got to go there in the morning to give her old man an injection.

Luke won't be there, and the old boy's pretty dozy. I could have a look round Luke's room—very quick like. Mind, it's not the sort of thing I reckon on doing, but this is an emergency.'

'Would you?' breathed Mair. 'Oh, good for you, Evadne.'

'Come back tomorrow,' said Evadne. 'Elevenish.'

At half past ten the next morning they were waiting outside the cottage. It was a warm, sunny day. The pond sparkled and the swallows on the telegraph wires chattered and preened themselves. Children played by garden gates, but the faces of the older people were sullen and unfriendly. There had been no further tampering with the lane: the policeman still stood by the churchyard wall.

'Never mind,' said Mair happily, 'it'll soon be over. If Evadne finds it then we can take it back to the wood, and tell Mr Tranter it's turned up, and Goacher can come home and everything'll be all right.'

'And Luke won't be able to do a thing,' Peter added in triumph.

'Goacher'll have to hide it somewhere different, of course. And never show it to anyone again.'

It all sounded very satisfactory.

At last Evadne appeared, hurrying past the pub. The children waved, and waited with expectant faces.

'Well?' said Peter, as they followed her into the cottage.

'Sorry, duckie,' said Evadne. 'Not a sausage, I'm afraid. It wasn't there. I felt awful, I don't mind telling you, walking into someone else's place, especially since we might be wrong about it. He's only got a tiny room, with a chest and a wardrobe, and it's not there. I looked really properly.'

There was an unhappy silence. 'Never mind,' said Peter at last. 'You tried, anyway.'

'I'm sure we're not wrong,' said Mair in a desperate voice. 'I'm *sure* it's him. We heard him talking to the

Tranters once—about money—and he was horrible. And if Betsy says he knew where it was . . .'

'He's a nasty piece of work all right,' said Evadne thoughtfully. 'He's been in trouble before, too, I know. It's the sort of thing he could well do.'

'We'll follow him,' said Mair. 'Night and day. Never let him out of our sight.'

Peter looked doubtful, and Evadne said warningly, 'Now you be careful how you go. You don't want to tangle with a character like Luke. They're a rough lot, some of those boys.'

'But we're the only people who could get it back.'

Peter said again, 'I don't see how we could. Honestly, Mair.'

They set off for home, Mair walking a few paces ahead, her hands thrust in her pockets and her face set in a sullen scowl. Peter knew this kind of mood and said nothing.

When they reached the main road she turned suddenly left instead of right towards the estate.

'Hey! Where are you going?'

'I'm going to the garage. I want to see if he's there. Don't come if you don't want to.'

Peter hesitated, then with a sigh he followed her down the road.

The garage extended each side of the main road, a hundred yards or so beyond the last house in the village. On one side was the forecourt, with petrol pumps, a car-inspection ramp and a glass-fronted office. On the other side was an enormous garage with double doors, big enough to hold two or three lorries—the repair shop.

Mair paused opposite the pumps, behind a bus shelter, and stood watching. Cars stopped for petrol and were filled by an elderly man. In the office another man could be seen through the glass, doing something at a desk. A van was straddled at the top of the ramp, and from underneath came the sound of hammering.

'Can't see him,' said Peter.

'Shut up. Look over there.' Somebody in blue overalls came out from under the van on the ramp, and began wheeling a tyre away from a pile at one end of the forecourt.

'Yes. That's him.'

They watched. Luke moved some tyres around, went in and out of the office, checked oil and water for a driver, and vanished again under the van on the ramp.

Peter grew restive. 'Look, we can't just sit here all day watching him. It won't help.'

'I shall if I want to,' said Mair obstinately. 'You go if you like.'

'He's not going to bring it out and wave it around, you know.'

'I never said he would, stupid.'

They stood in silence, Mair staring intently at the van. Peter sat down on the seat in the bus shelter. After ten minutes he said, 'I think I'll go home, if you really don't mind.' Mair said nothing, and he set off down the road. When he looked back, she was still standing in the same place, her hands in the pockets of her jeans, hair all over her face.

Luke spent a long time under the van. Finally he came out, rolled it off the ramp, and wiped his hands on a rag. The man in the office came out and shouted 'Tea's up.' Luke disappeared into a room behind the office. There was no one in sight now.

Mair sidled along beside the hedge, watching the office all the time, until she reached the entrance of the repair shop. With a final glance behind she slipped inside, and stood, shivering slightly in the oil-smelling gloom, listening. Everything was quite quiet. There didn't seem to be anyone else around. The place was full of cars, one or two of them jacked up as though in process of repair, the rest parked along the walls. It was rather dark, the only daylight filtering through from dirty skylights overhead. There were piles of tyres, and shelves of oily cans and tins of paint. A couple of bicycles leant against one wall.

Mair edged furtively along the wall, straining her ears all the time. Lorries kept grinding past outside, drowning all other sounds. Then suddenly she saw it, pushed into a gap between two cars half-way down the garage: the motor-bike with crossed flags on the rear mudguard. She hesitated for a moment, and went back to the entrance to peer cautiously across the road. There was still no one about in the forecourt. She went quickly back to the motor-bike, her heart thumping, and began to examine it. There were two leather satchels hanging from either side of the pillion seat behind the saddle. Shaking all over now, she un-buckled them one by one and thrust her hand inside. One was empty. The other held a torch and a packet of sand-wiches. Behind the pillion seat a bright yellow plastic cape was rolled up in a tight bundle and strapped down. With a quick glance over her shoulder she began to unstrap it. Outside, a heavy lorry thundered past.

The buckle was stiff: it took her several seconds to get it undone. At last she had the bundle of plastic free and started to unroll it. She knew almost at once that she had been right—there was something hard inside. More excited than frightened, she gave it a final shake, and the chalice rolled out onto the oily concrete floor of the garage. She bent over it: the tiny gargoyle faces stared up at her.

She didn't hear the scrape of his shoe until he was almost on top of her: he must have come in very quietly. She dropped the chalice with a stifled scream and shot back-wards, staring at him in terror.

Luke picked up the chalice and thrust it into a pocket of his overall. Then, without speaking, he began to advance slowly towards her. Mair backed away, almost tripping over a length of steel pipe on the floor. Luke was between

135

her and the open door. She edged round a car and he followed her, still saying nothing.

'Let me get out,' she said suddenly, 'or I'll scream.'

'There ain't no one here.'

They both stopped, facing each other. Mair was shaking so much that she thought she might fall.

'You leave my stuff alone, see,' he said, 'or I'll make you sorry for it.'

'It isn't yours,' said Mair, with a rush of boldness. 'You've got no business with it. Give it back. It's your fault there's all this trouble in the village.'

He grinned, watching her with his small, close-together eyes. 'It ain't my fault if they're a lot 'o fools, is it? And who's to say I got it. There ain't no one as'll say so.'

There was a sound on the pavement outside and Luke looked over his shoulder for a moment. Mair darted behind another car and ran for the entrance. He made a lunge at her as she passed, but missed her, and she was outside again and running away down the road towards the village, with cars swishing past and a woman pushing a shopping-trolley staring after her in surprise.

Ten

ALL THE way back to the house, panting and stumbling, pushing her hair out of her eyes with a shaking hand, she was busy thinking. It was curious that you could think quite clearly even with your heart thumping fit to burst. I know he's got it, and he knows I know he's got it, but what on earth are we going to do about it? Nobody's going to believe me except Peter, and maybe Evadne, and Goacher of course. Evadne's grown-up—she could tell the police, but they'd say: how do you know? and she'd have to admit she hadn't actually seen for herself, but that I told her, and we'd be back where we started. The only advantage we've got is that Luke's got no one on his side at all, and if we could get it off him there wouldn't be a thing he could do about it.

So we've got to get it from him somehow. On our own.

They're a rough lot, some of those boys, Evadne said. I 'spose he mightn't hurt me: I'm a girl. But he'd go for Pete, and Pete's much smaller than him. He's got nasty eyes. Come to that, I daresay he wouldn't mind having a go at me too. Maybe he's got a knife. Boys like that do sometimes.

He's got a motor-bike, too, to get away on.

We haven't got anything. Except, perhaps . . . I wonder . . .

Peter was whole-heartedly impressed. He didn't even try to conceal it.

'Gosh Mair, well done! Weren't you scared stiff? I think I would have been. When you were there all alone with him?'

'Yes, I was. Petrified.' She too could afford to be honest.

There was a pause: then Peter said, 'We'll have to do something. Now. Today. Now he knows we know he's got it he'll be trying to get rid of it as quick as he can.'

Mair nodded, still breathless. 'Yes. Except that he didn't think I was anything much to bother about—I could tell that. All the same, you're right. But listen—I had an idea when I was coming back.'

She explained.

Peter interrupted in a shocked voice before she'd finished. 'We can't hunt him with dogs—like police or something. We just couldn't. Besides, Fang and the Bitch are pretty wild: they might really hurt him. And we couldn't control them.'

'Oh, do let me *finish*. Of course we're not going to let them really get at him. We'll just have them with us—like a sort of threat. It's fair. He's got a motor-bike, and he's much stronger than us: so we'll have the dogs.'

'But how are we going to cope with them? They're not the sort of dogs you trail around with you on a lead.'

138

'No, we couldn't. But Goacher could. We'll have to get him.'

They planned carefully. Peter was to go off as quickly as he could to find Goacher and bring him to the village. Mair would watch the garage, keeping well out of sight, to make sure Luke spent the afternoon there and didn't go off anywhere. It was now nearly one o'clock.

'What about dinner?'

'We'll ask Mum for sandwiches. We're going out for the rest of the day. Bird-watching.'

'What if Goacher won't come?'

'He will for you,' said Mair. 'He likes you. And if you can, make him understand how important it is. But for goodness sake hurry up. Luke'll stop work at some point, and then we've all got to be together, following him. You and me and Goacher and the dog: perhaps just one of them would be better than two.'

Peter had worked out a kind of plan. It was no good trying to do anything while Luke was in the village, with other people around. They must, somehow, try to shadow him until he was on his own somewhere and they could hope to frighten him sufficiently to make him give up the chalice, or be able to take it from him. They must try also to separate him from the motor-bike, with which he would always be in the strong position of being able to get away quicker than they could ever hope to follow him.

'The only thing is to surprise him,' said Mair, 'and we might be able to do that because I bet he thought he'd scared me off and seen the last of me.'

Leaving Mair crouched behind the hedge facing the garage, peering through a strategic gap, Peter set off to find Goacher. At least this time he could head straight for the ruined house, but even so he reckoned it would take him at least an hour, there and back. He hurried through the wood and out into the fields. It seemed a long time before he was at the top of the hill, looking down over the valley, with the copse near Millfield House a green blob in the distance, and even longer to cross the valley and the road and the stream and make his way up the far side towards the wood. He went round the edge of it, to save time, and skirted the bowl of the quarry, and then at last the clump of chestnuts and the house were in sight. He approached cautiously: the place still seemed sinister and watchful, even though he knew it held nothing more alarming than cows, sheep, and, he hoped, Goacher.

Somehow it had never crossed his mind that Goacher might have gone, so that it came as an unpleasant shock to find the summer-house empty. He looked round wildly thinking: oh, help, what if I can't find him! And then, with a rush of relief, he heard a short, sharp bark from somewhere in the fields beyond the tangle that had once been a garden. He ran across the grass calling 'It's all right—it's only me, Goacher.'

Goacher was sitting on the bank of a shallow stream, staring sadly into the water, with Fang patrolling restlessly up and down beside him.

Peter sat down and began to explain. Goacher listened, various expressions contorting his round face: anger, anxiety, confusion.

'So we want you to come back with me,' Peter finished, 'and bring Fang, and help us to get it back from him.'

'Fang'll tear 'un up,' said Goacher with relish. 'I only got to tell 'e to and e'd tear 'un to pieces.'

'That's just what we don't want,' said Peter hastily. 'We just want to have Fang there. Is Luke scared of Fang?'

'Everyone be scared of Fang.'

'But he'd do what you said? Fang, I mean. He wouldn't attack anyone unless you told him to?'

Goacher shook his head. He seemed almost regretful.

'He's a bad 'un, that Luke. He tricked me, he did. Made me show him the Thing. Said he wouldn't never touch it. He tricked me.'

140

'Well, that can't be helped now. But will you come?'

Goacher looked worried again. He scrubbed at his eyes nervously with a stubby-fingered hand. 'I'm frightened of 'em—the people. They'll be thinkin' it was me took the Thing. I don't want 'em to see me.'

'You can stay hidden. And that's why we've got to get it back: so no one'll think you took it any more.'

Goacher brightened. He got to his feet and set off across the field, with Fang loping at his heels as though attached to him by an invisible cord. Peter hurried after them.

For Mair, the afternoon was apparently interminable. Lying on her stomach, tickled by grass and crawled on by unidentifiable things that she had to ignore unless she was to stand up shuddering and give herself away, she kept looking at her watch to find that what had seemed five minutes had in fact been barely two. At first she hadn't been able to locate Luke, which had given her a sinking feeling, but then he'd emerged from the repair shed to fetch something from the office, and returned there almost at once, so that although he was out of sight she could hear him moving about and occasionally hammering, or tuning an engine. She was bound to see him come out. Once a lorry stopped for a time outside the garage, obscuring her view of the door, and she got into a fret of anxiety in case he should choose that moment to leave. But when the lorry had gone she could still hear sounds from inside, and relaxed again.

At last she heard a noise behind her, and looked round to see Peter and Goacher making their way stealthily across the field. She looked at her watch: it was still only four o'clock. The others joined her behind the hedge and the three of them lay there, watching, with Fang crouched beside Goacher, motionless, his head between his paws, only the tip of his tail twitching from time to time and his eyes shining yellow when the light caught them.

Half past four. Quarter to five. Five o'clock. At five past

five Luke came out of the garage, wheeling his motor-bike. The yellow cape, wrapped up, was strapped once again behind the pillion.

He got on to the bike and kicked the starter. The engine spluttered and fired. 'He's going,' said Mair, in anguish. 'We won't be able to keep up.'

'It's all right,' hissed Peter, 'I thought he would. But he'll go back to the village to change out of his overalls, won't he? Put on the leather jacket and all that stuff.'

Luke roared down the road. As soon as he was out of sight the children and Goacher hurried along behind the hedge in the direction of the village. But once the houses were in sight, and gardens with people, and open doors, Goacher began to whimper and hang back.

'I ain't comin' no nearer.'

They were just coming up to the entrance to one of the narrow lanes that radiated from the village green like the spokes of a wheel, ending abruptly where the fields began. There were a few cottages, facing each other, at either side of it, and then, just at the edge of the field, a hayrick.

'Get behind the rick,' said Peter, 'and wait there. And for goodness sake keep a tight told of Fang. Don't let him move an inch. Stay there till we come. We'll go to Evadne's and watch from there.'

Goacher nodded obediently and slipped behind the rick. Peter and Mair made their way down the lane to the green, casting anxious looks all round them. There was no sign of Luke until they reached the green. And then Mair pointed silently. At the far side of the pond, leaning against a garden fence outside the cottage he lived in, was the motor-bike. So far, so good.

They crept round to Evadne's back door and Peter banged urgently on the window. Evadne came almost at once.

They told her everything that had happened, both together, almost shouting, so that she had to keep saying

'What? What did he do? For heaven's sake talk one at a time.'

When things were quieter they all three went to the window that overlooked the green. Luke's motor-bike was still leaning against the fence. The other motor-bike boys had started to gather under the oak-tree, drifting up in ones and twos. Apart from that there was no one much around, but Mair, looking over towards the pub, saw a man's face appear at the window and stay for a moment, watching, before it disappeared inside again.

'They're getting ready,' said Evadne quietly. 'Another hour or two, when the cars begin to come . . .'

After a few minutes Luke came out of the cottage, slamming the door behind him. He wore his studded leather jacket and the huge, wide-wristed gauntlets, with goggles pushed up on to his forehead. He rode the bike over to join the other boys in a leisurely way, and then stood with them, talking and smoking. The yellow cape was strapped behind the pillion.

'What if he's not got the chalice with him?' said Mair, tense.

'He's carried it around up to now. Why should he stop? Specially since this afternoon.'

'The thing is,' Peter went on after a moment, 'that we can't do anything while he's with the others. We've got to get him away from them.'

At the far end of the green, by the church, there were two policemen standing, hands clasped behind their backs.

'Let me think,' said Evadne. 'I believe there's something I could do. You say Goacher's at the end of that lane with the dog?'

'Yes.'

'I see. Just wait a bit, then. Watch them. They'll stay around a while yet, they always do.'

Like swallows gathering on a telegraph wire, swooping off on short excursions in twos and threes, only to reassemble a moment later, the bike boys would dart off every now and then to roar round the green, or go up the lane and back, or down one of the side lanes, and then gather again at their centre under the oak-tree. Evadne and the children watched them closely. They had their goggles and helmets on now: evidently the time was drawing near for the evening migration. But Luke was still distinguishable by the crossed flags on the back of his bike. Every now and then he, too, would make a noisy tour of the village. Twice he went down the lane at the end of which Goacher was hiding behind the rick. Down to the end, a burst of revs on the engine, a pebble-scattering turn, and back to the oak tree.

'That's it!' said Evadne, eyes sparkling. 'Now listen. This is what we'll do . . .'

Two minutes later Peter crept out of the back door and made his way round the back of the village to where Goacher was hiding. Then he returned, and he and Mair strolled, as inconspicuously as they could, to a point near where the lane to the field joined the green. At the same time Evadne came out of her cottage and drove her car round until it stood a few yards from the entrance to the lane, near the children. Then she sat in it, the engine running, apparently going over some papers.

The bike boys took no notice. They were evidently very close to leaving: the evening quiet was shattered by the din of their engines. A small group of them swept round the green, up the lane and back again. And then came Luke, alone, faceless in helmet and goggles, like a mechanised robot. He circled the green, twice, while the children clutched each other in excitement and Evadne's hands moved to the steering-wheel of the car. The other boys had already roared away up the lane past the church and out into the main road. Would he follow them? He seemed about to, and then another robot figure cruised past the children and Evadne, into the lane, to the end, turned, and

144

came out. Luke swerved, changed direction, and roared past them.

Evadne had moved before he reached the end of the lane. When he turned, skidding on the stones, the car was completely blocking the other end, boxing him in. He ground to a stop, and seemed about to shout something, and at the same moment Goacher rose from where he had been squatting inside a garden gate. He was holding Fang by a fold of loose skin at his neck, and the animal was growling and straining. Luke hesitated and took a step backwards.

Peter and Mair heard Goacher say 'Fang be goin' to get you, Luke. I be goin' to let 'un go.'

Luke swore, and stepped back again, letting the motor-bike fall to the ground. It lay on its side, throbbing. Fang crouched, as though to spring.

'Give it to me,' said Goacher thickly. 'Give me the Thing. Or I'll let 'un get you.'

'No!' shouted Mair, panic-stricken. 'Don't let Fang go! Remember what we said.'

Goacher hesitated, and half turned, and as he did so Luke stooped, wrenched the yellow cape from the bike, and ran, out of the lane and into the field beyond.

They were after him, all three of them, pelting down the lane, slipping and sliding on the loose surface, with Fang running nose to ground, ears flattened.

'I wouldn't have let 'un go,' grumbled Goacher, panting. 'It were to frighten 'un.'

'Well, it did,' said Mair. 'It worked all right.'

In the field, they could just see Luke's running figure weaving between the yellow blocks of straw. He turned once to look over his shoulder and changed direction. He was heading for the main road.

'Don't let him get to the road!' cried Peter. 'He could get away there. Run!'

But Luke had too good a start. They had no hope of catching up with him before he reached the road.

'Could Fang head him off?' said Mair urgently. 'Like the rabbit with the hawk?'

Goacher said something sharply to the dog, and he sprang away with a great bound and began to run low along the ground, fast, near the hedge. He would cut Luke off in time. Luke saw him, hesitated a moment, and then swerved and began to run away from the road, deeper into the field.

'He's going to circle round the village,' said Peter. 'Call Fang back!'

At the far side of the field a tractor moved slowly along beside the hedge, bright blue against the yellow stubble, the driver motionless in his seat, like a figure on a model. For a moment Mair wondered if Luke would run to him, or call for help, and then, instantly, she knew that he wouldn't. This was between him and them: no one else would come into it. The village, and the tractor, and the road, were another world, a different dimension. All that mattered were the four figures running in the evening sunshine across the fields behind the village, and the dog that ran beside them.

They were between Luke and the village, and between Luke and the road. There were two ways he could go: into the lane that ran down to the farm, or into the wood. He did not hesitate: as soon as he reached the edge of the wood they saw him duck under the wire and vanish into the undergrowth. Goacher let out a cry of triumph.

'We'll get 'un there! No one knows the wood like I does.'

They were under the wire and into the wood two or three minutes behind Luke. It was like going from daylight to dusk: this was the very thickest part, and the sunshine came only dimly through the thick layer of leaves overhead, the sparkle muted, almost quenched. It was quite quiet, the only noise their own feet stumbling through bushes and fallen branches.

'Follow Fang!' said Goacher. 'Fang can scent 'un.'

146

The dog wove in and out of the trees, vanishing sometimes into the undergrowth, pausing occasionally to throw
up his head and sniff. There was a dark shadow all down
his back where the hairs were standing straight up. But a
dog hunting by scent goes slowly, slower than his quarry.
He dodges about, distracted by other smells, pausing to
analyse what he finds: his quarry can run straight. Every
minute they were falling further behind Luke. Presently
they emerged from this dense part of the wood into the
more open places, where bluebells and spurge had carpeted
the ground earlier in the year and now bracken and willow-
herb grew, waist high. It was possible to see some way
ahead, and the sunlight came striking down all around
them. Fang paused for a moment, confused, and then nosed
around in the grass and seemed to find a positive line again,
for he bounded away eagerly down one of the trails
between the trees. Goacher was close behind, followed by
Peter.

Mair was out of breath. Her ears were buzzing, and red
spots came and went before her eyes. I can't go on, she
thought, I must slow down, just for a moment. I can catch
them up. She slowed to a jog-trot, taking gulps of air. That's
better—I'll be all right in a minute.

And then her foot caught in a root or tangle of bramble
and she felt herself falling headlong. She flung out her arms
to save herself, but too late. She hit the ground with a stun-
ning thud, banging her head on a stone, and rolled over
on to her back with everything spinning in black circles
and the wood noises coming and going in waves.

She lay there for several minutes, not unconscious, but
not interested in getting to her feet either. She lay with
her eyes open, staring up at the trees, and the sunlight
crackled and sizzled and blinked at her through the leaves
like reflections on water, so that at one moment she was
sure she was suspended face-down, spread-eagled, staring
down into a rippling green lake. And then, sickeningly,

everything swung and she was the right way up again. And then the noises began to come, the people shuffling past, barefoot on a dusty path, and the soft clop of cattle, and creak of a cart, and was that the sound of children playing? Clear little voices, somewhere further away. No bells, she thought, dizzily. Must be the wrong time of day.

Another noise, more distinct, made her lift her head a little and take her eyes off the leaves. She looked along her own body, down the track, at knee-height, and saw a pair of legs, standing.

'That's funny: I've never actually seen people before. Only noises, and smells.'

The legs moved, and Mair's eyes travelled up them, to thin hips, and gauntleted hands hanging down at either side, and a studded leather jacket.

She shot to her feet with a scream and began to retreat down the path shouting 'Peter! Goacher! Quick! He's here!'

But they must have been out of earshot. When her shouts died away the wood was quiet, and Luke was walking slowly towards her. And there was something in his hand: something shiny that caught the light.

Mair screamed again and turned and ran, crashing through leaves and branches, and through the noise she was making herself, and her thudding heart, she was sure she could hear the crash of following footsteps.

And then suddenly there was something quick, fawn-coloured, leaping between the trees towards her. Fang! no, The Bitch. They'd forgotten all about her. For a confused moment Mair thought the dog was going to spring at her, but she slid past, growling in her throat, and then stopped, hackles up, snarling and baring her teeth. Mair stopped too, and turned.

Luke and the dog were facing each other, ten or fifteen yards apart. The dog was still snarling, but she looked back at Mair uncertainly and Mair thought: she doesn't know what to do—she knows she mustn't attack unless she's told to.

Does Luke know that?

He hesitated for a moment, and then he turned and ran.

Mair plunged off in the opposite direction, The Bitch shadowing her among the trees. She shouted and called incoherently, and after a few minutes her shouts were answered as Peter and Goacher came running down the path and, gasping and panting, she was able to tell them what had happened.

Again Luke had several minutes start, and the dogs took minutes more to pick up his scent. And then, when they had it, they seemed to run in circles, crossing the path, in and out of the undergrowth, hither and thither.

'What are they doing?' said Peter despairingly. 'He can't have gone in circles like that. He'd have kept to the path.'

'Scent must be bad,' said Goacher. 'They be pickin' up other trails—rabbit and badger and that. It be hard for 'em when scent be lyin' badly.'

But at last the dogs led them to one of the exits from the wood. It was the same side of the farm, though further to the west, and the land sloped gently down from the wood into the same shallow valley that sheltered World's End Farm. Indeed, distantly, just visible in a fold of the land, they could see a part of the farm buildings. They climbed out of the wood into a grassy field, and the dogs darted about, searching for the scent. Peter and Mair searched the horizon, but there was no one in sight.

The dogs found the line and began to run across the field towards a stile at the far end. They were going fast now and it was all the children could do to keep up. At the stile they hesitated, casting here and there along the hedge and into the next field, and then set off again confidently across another field. Still they could not sight Luke.

They must have run half a mile like this, down the slope

and into the flat bottom of the valley, where a narrow stream winding through willows and reeds gave the dogs several minutes confusion as they cast up and down the bank to find the point where Luke had crossed it and continued over the field on the far side. And now they had reached a piece of countryside where several fields had been thrown into one vast one, of forty or fifty acres, rolling away on either side and ahead in a gentle slope to the rise at the far side of the valley. It had been a field of barley, harvested now, with green already striping the stubble as the grass grew again, and spotted with straw-bales. At the far side, a road wound along the edge of the field and up to the top of the rise: they could just see the movement of cars far away in the distance.

'If he gets to the road,' said Peter uneasily, 'we'll lose him. He could thumb a lift or something before we can catch up.'

And then they saw him, far away, a small figure running through the stubble in the distance. Running towards the road.

Goacher had stopped suddenly. He was standing staring intently upwards into the cloudless sky, one hand shading his eyes and pushing the yellow hair off his forehead.

'Come on,' Peter shouted impatiently, 'he's miles ahead as it is.'

Goacher pointed upwards. 'It be old bird,' he said with interest. 'He be lookin' for food, I reckon.'

High above them, a small black shape hung in the sky. Then it swept round effortlessly in a circle and hung again, lower.

'Oh, Goacher, *please*,' said Mair. 'There isn't time to bother with the hawk now. We're going to lose the dogs— do come on.'

'I be goin' to call 'un down,' said Goacher obstinately. 'It be my bird.' His leather glove was slung from a loop on his belt and he put it on. Astonishingly the bird circled again, and began to descend in diminishing circles, as though drawn to the glove by a magnet. Mair had a sudden startling vision of what a hawk's-eye view of the landscape must be: a flattened map full of clamouring detail, movements here and there, a rabbit, a mouse, and now the glove to which it must come because that was what it had always done.

The hawk dropped on to the glove and settled, gripping with its talons, the orange eye glaring.

'Come on,' said Mair, in anguish. The distant figure of Luke was receding every moment, and the dogs were ploughing on across the field, noses down, weaving from side to side as they followed his trail.

Peter was looking at the hawk. Then he glanced away across the field at the running man and cried in excitement, 'Goacher! Send him up again—quick! And take your glove off.'

Goacher stared stupidly. 'Send old bird up again?'

'Yes, yes! But quickly!'

Mair gaped.

Goacher swung his fist back and threw the bird up. It soared, up and up.

'Take the glove off. Throw it away. And run.' Peter began tearing across the stubble after the dogs and the man.

Bewildered, Goacher threw down the glove and stumbled after him. And at the same moment Mair saw what must happen and clapped her hand to her mouth.

The hawk climbed and hung in the bright air. It soared for a moment or two, and then began to glide down, away from them, away from Goacher, and towards Luke. Luke, running hard, did not see it, until he must suddenly have heard the rush of its great wings almost upon him, and then he turned and flung up his gauntleted arms to ward it off. And as they approached, they saw him stumbling backwards, terrified, as the hawk flapped round him,

151

confused, diving again and again at the familiar gloves that tried to push it away instead of offering the security it sought. Again and again it swooped at him, until he tripped and fell to the ground, shouting and trying to cover his face and head with his arms, and still the hawk flapped and hovered, trying desperately to get a footing on the glove that would not keep still.

Goacher was shouting at the dogs, calling them back. Peter covered the last fifty yards in a wild sprint, grabbed the yellow cape which Luke had dropped as he fell, felt the hard lump of the chalice inside, turned and fled back across the field, calling the others to follow him.

They did not look back until they reached the stream. Luke had got up and was running again towards the road, shielding his head with his hands, and the hawk was circling round and round, until finally it flew off and settled disconsolately on a tree-stump.

'That won't do 'un no good,' said Goacher crossly, ' 'e'll be shy of the glove now. I'll have to teach 'un all over again.'

Eleven

WHEN THEY got back to the village they found Evadne in a fever of impatience. It was past six, and clearly the men of Charlton were busy with last-minute preparations to repel the evening invasion. They were going into the pub in ones and twos, purposefully, and from time to time a face would appear at the window, staring out, and then vanish again. And already two of the younger men were strolling self-consciously up and down, fingering the heavy staves that they carried over one shoulder. All around the green, windows opened and closed, and children were being called into the houses.

Evadne brushed aside their excited explanations. She grabbed the chalice, and Goacher, and bundled them both into her car.

'Where are you going?' panted Peter, tugging at the door-handle. He had somehow envisaged a triumphal progress round the green, brandishing the chalice.

'To get old George Tranter, that's what. He can come up here and make it plain to them all that there's no need for any more fuss. Since it all began down at World's End he's the one to do it. Remind them what it was all about in the first place and tell them to pull themselves together.'

'Do hurry,' said Mair nervously. Something that looked suspiciously like a rifle protruded for a moment from the pub window, and was withdrawn.

The children waited, anxiously watching the lane from the main road. So far no car had driven down it.

At last Evadne came back, bucketing round the corner.

She stopped at the pub, and Mr Tranter got out of the car and walked slowly up to the door. His shoulders were hunched and Mair, catching sight of his face for a moment, thought he looked embarrassed. He paused briefly, and then pushed the door open and went inside.

For a long time nothing happened. The pub door remained closed: nobody came or went. And then suddenly a window was thrown open and from inside came sounds of laughter, and glasses clinking. And then one of the men came out and walked quickly across the green to one of the cottages and went inside. A few minutes later a woman came out and called at a neighbouring cottage. And then, gradually, like a place coming to life in the early morning, Charlton Underwood began to hum with activity. Children played under the oak tree, women talked across garden fences, Tom Craddock and some of the other men came out of the pub with brimming beer-mugs and stood in the sunshine beside the pond.

When the first car did come down the lane nobody took any notice. Some people got out and walked round the green.

'Evenin',' said Tom Craddock. 'Nice bit o' weather we're havin'.'

The visitors looked faintly disappointed. After another minute or two they left.

Evadne and the children stood watching. 'I see the young Leacocks have made a smart recovery,' said Evadne with a grin. 'And, dear me, if that isn't Miss Barton taking a turn round the pond. She couldn't put a foot to the ground yesterday.'

'What about Betsy?' said Mair.

'She'll be fine now. She's nearly over the mumps anyway—be up and about in another day or two. Young Luke's got something coming to him, though, I can tell you, when Mr Tranter gets his hands on him.'

After a while Mr Tranter came out of the pub and set

off towards the main road, after much back-slapping and shouts of 'Cheero, then, George,' from the other men. He looked once in the direction of the children and they had the feeling that he had seen them, but preferred not to admit it.

This, thought Peter, is going to be one of those things that nobody ever says anything about once it's over and done with.

The children didn't go straight home. Neither of them said anything but with one accord they headed for the wood. There was just one more thing to do. They went across the field, where the cows were being brought in for milking, fanned out over the bright grass, ambling unhurriedly towards the gate. The wood was just starting to throw its evening shadow across the field, down the long backbones of the old ridge and furrow. It was very still, and quiet, though the tops of the trees swayed and shivered.

Before they reached the edge of the wood there was a crashing in the undergrowth and the dogs came bounding out, their tails waving in welcome. Tar, who'd never entirely taken to them, retreated to the hedge and began to take a great interest in a rabbit burrow. A moment or two later Goacher's yellow head appeared among the branches and he climbed through the fence.

'I bin watchin' for you,' he said.

'Goacher,' said Peter, 'where's the Thing?'

Goacher looked round furtively. 'I hidden 'un,' he said. 'I hidden 'un in a new place. Come, and you can see 'un.'

The children stared at him in silence and said nothing. Then all of a sudden Goacher's expression changed. He looked away uncomfortably.

'No,' he said. 'I ain't goin' to show 'un to you. I ain't goin' to show 'un to anyone no more. It be hidden for always now.'

Peter grinned with satisfaction. 'That's it, Goacher,' he said, 'that's right.'

Goacher squinted at them craftily, pleased with himself.

'We'd better go home,' said Mair. 'What is it we're supposed to have been doing all day? Bird-watching?'

They turned away and began to walk back to the village.

'We'll go and see the Tranters tomorrow,' said Peter.

Mair nodded. She turned and looked back. There was no sign of Goacher and the dogs. The wood had swallowed them up again, an enfolding green sea, just as it had quietly taken Astercote, all those many years ago, and hidden the tumbled stones of the houses, and the cobbled street, and the pointing spire of the church, and spread grass over the stones as they crumbled, and let the thrusting growth of young trees fell the church walls and give them to the concealing bramble and thorn. Shadows ran across the wood, like the wind ruffling the fur of a sleeping animal, and as Mair turned her back on it the distant sound of the bells followed her across the field and then died away on the evening air.

Also by Penelope Lively

THE GHOST OF THOMAS KEMPE

Winner of the Carnegie Medal

When the Harrisons move to an old cottage in Oxfordshire they are beset by small domestic disasters. Naturally they assume James is up to his tricks again – how can he tell them he is being plagued by the ghost of a meddling seventeenth-century sorcerer, bent on making James his apprentice?

James tries desperately to circumvent the sorcerer's malicious activities, but it is only when he uncovers the reason for Thomas Kempe's sudden reappearance that he finds a way to lay the ghost forever . . .

'A bouncing, hilarious story, first-class fun from beginning to end.'

Books and Bookmen

'A sunny story of the supernatural . . . observed with exactitude and humour.'

The Guardian

Penelope Lively

THE HOUSE IN NORHAM GARDENS

Fourteen-year-old Clare lives with her two aunts at 40 Norham Gardens, a vast, eccentric Victorian house whose rooms are filled with old papers, old clothes and antiquated furniture. For Clare it is a shadowy, disturbing time. She has discovered a shield in the attic, brought back from New Guinea by her great-grandfather. Her dreams are haunted by images of New Guinea and it eventually falls to Clare to lay the ghost of an encounter between a Victorian anthropologist and a Stone Age tribe living in New Guinea seventy years ago.

'memorable descriptions, precise images, some splendidly observed characters, a story to enjoy and ponder.'

Times Educational Supplement

'A rare achievement.'

Evening Standard

Penelope Lively

THE WHISPERING KNIGHTS

William, Susie and Martha concoct a witches' brew. They don't expect anything to happen but, as they chant their spell over a bubbling cauldron, an uneasy feeling creeps over them.

An evil spirit, Morgan le Fay, has been aroused, and mischief and destruction is brought to the village. The children have to fight Morgan themselves, leading her finally to the only enemy that matches her strength – the Whispering Knights.

'Penelope Lively is a natural storyteller with a gift for holding attention . . . the events are vivid, exciting but always believable. Guaranteed to succeed as a gripping adventure story . . .'

Books for Keeps

'outstandingly good . . . beautifully contains the different characters . . . springing direct from the author's genius.'

New Statesman

Penelope Lively

THE WILD HUNT OF HAGWORTHY

Lucy looks forward to summer in the country and to renewing her friendship with Caroline, Louise and Kester, the Blacksmith's son. But soon after she arrives, Lucy is troubled by the news that the ancient and long-forgotten Horn Dance is to be revived again at the summer fête.

As the participants rehearse in their old costumes and antlered masks, Lucy feels that sinister forces from the past are being unleashed and that the ghostly Wild Hunt will return – bringing with it a terrible danger . . .

'Narrative explodes into speed and terror before the shadows are beaten back.'

The Guardian

'Telling descriptions of the Somerset countryside and excellent, funny modern dialogue combine with a very real supernatural to make a powerful whole.'

The Times

'most compelling.'

Birmingham Post

A Selected List of Fiction from Mammoth

While every effort is made to keep prices low, it is sometimes necessary to increase prices at short notice. Mandarin Paperbacks reserves the right to show new retail prices on covers which may differ from those previously advertised in the text or elsewhere.

The prices shown below were correct at the time of going to press.

☐	7497 0978 2	**Trial of Anna Cotman**	Vivien Alcock	£2.99
☐	7497 1771 8	**Kezzie**	Theresa Breslin	£2.99
☐	7497 1794 7	**Born of the Sun**	Gillian Cross	£3.50
☐	7497 1066 7	**The Animals of Farthing Wood**	Colin Dann	£3.99
☐	7497 1823 4	**White Peak Farm**	Berlie Doherty	£2.99
☐	7497 0184 6	**The Summer House Loon**	Anne Fine	£2.99
☐	7497 0443 8	**Fast From the Gate**	Michael Hardcastle	£2.50
☐	7497 1784 X	**Listen to the Dark**	Maeve Henry	£2.99
☐	7497 0136 6	**I Am David**	Anne Holm	£3.99
☐	7497 1473 5	**Charmed Life**	Diana Wynne Jones	£3.50
☐	7497 1664 9	**Hiding Out**	Elizabeth Laird	£3.50
☐	7497 0791 7	**The Ghost of Thomas Kempe**	Penelope Lively	£3.50
☐	7497 1754 8	**The War of Jenkins' Ear**	Michael Morpurgo	£3.50
☐	7497 0831 X	**The Snow Spider**	Jenny Nimmo	£2.99
☐	7497 1772 6	**The Panic Wall**	Alick Rowe	£3.50
☐	7497 0656 2	**Journey of 1000 Miles**	Ian Strachan	£2.99
☐	7497 0796 8	**Kingdom by the Sea**	Robert Westall	£3.50

All these books are available at your bookshop or newsagent, or can be ordered direct from the address below. Just tick the titles you want and fill in the form below.

Cash Sales Department, PO Box 5, Rushden, Northants NN10 6YX.
Fax: 01933 414047 : Phone: 01933 414000.

Please send cheque, payable to 'Reed Book Services Ltd.', or postal order for purchase price quoted and allow the following for postage and packing:

£1.00 for the first book, 50p for the second; **FREE POSTAGE AND PACKING FOR THREE BOOKS OR MORE PER ORDER.**

NAME (Block letters) ....

ADDRESS ....

....

☐ I enclose my remittance for ....

☐ I wish to pay by Access/Visa Card Number ☐☐☐☐☐☐☐☐☐☐☐☐☐☐☐☐

Expiry Date ☐☐☐☐

Signature ....

Please quote our reference: MAND